WINTER'S BURN

The Springs—Four

ELENA AITKEN

Winter's Burn

Also by Elena Aitken

The Springs Series

Summer of Change

Falling Into Forever

Second Glances

Winter's Burn

Midnight Springs

She's Making A List

Summit of Desire

Summit of Seduction

Summit of Passion

Fighting For Forever

The Springs Collection: Volume 1

The Springs Collection: Volume 2

The Springs Collection: Volume 3

The Springs Complete Collection - Books 1-10

The McCormicks

Love in the Moment

Only for a Moment

One more Moment

In this Moment

From this Moment

Our Perfect Moment

Ever After

Choosing Happily Ever After

Needing Happily Ever After

Wanting Happily Ever After

Fighting Happily Ever After

Timber Creek

When We Left

When We Were Us

When We Began

When We Fell

Castle Mountain Lodge

Unexpected Gifts

Hidden Gifts

Unexpected Endings - Short Story

Mistaken Gifts

Secret Gifts

Goodbye Gifts

Tempting Gifts

Holiday Gifts

Promised Gifts

Accidental Gifts

The Castle Mountain Lodge Collection: Books 1-3

The Castle Mountain Lodge Collection: Books 4-6

The Castle Mountain Lodge Collection: Books 7-9

The Castle Mountain Lodge Complete Collection

Halfway Series

Halfway to Nowhere

Halfway in Between

Halfway to Christmas

Chapter One

BY THE TIME Beth Martin navigated her secondhand SUV up the icy mountain road to the Springs resort, she was ready to turn around and head back down. It was way too cold of a day to be at work, even if work was a luxury resort built around natural hot springs. Maybe she could find a moment to sneak off and absorb some heat from their steam, she thought as she parked her car.

Despite the urge to turn around and spend her day cuddled up under her quilt with a good book, nothing would keep Beth from work. Not only did she love her job as the staff physiotherapist at the resort, she was dammed lucky to have it and she knew it. She wouldn't be doing anything to screw up that opportunity any time soon.

She tugged the zipper of her parka up as far as it would go, made sure her knit cap was firmly in place and braced herself against the bitter wind and made her way as quickly to the staff entrance door as possible in her snowboots and thick coat. There were lots of advantages to living in the Rocky Mountains, but snowstorms in January weren't one of them. It didn't seem to matter how many winters she lived through in her hometown of Cedar Springs, she'd never get used to the storms that blew in over the mountains with what seemed like no warning at all.

In a whirl of snow and ice, Beth pushed through the door and into the back hallway. As soon as the door was closed behind her, she allowed herself a moment of rest and leaned back against the wall. Winter had a funny way of making you feel like you'd lived an entire day by eight in the morning. Or maybe it wasn't winter, but the battle she'd had with her daughter trying to get her out of the house. It's not that Jules was a bad kid—far from it. But at twelve, she definitely had a strong sense of what she wanted, and if those wants didn't coincide with Beth's ideas, it was a recipe for disaster. Or at least a morning that resulted in Beth needing a stiff drink with her coffee.

Beth pulled off her hood and shook her blond hair loose.

"Pretty nasty out there, hey?" Carmen, her friend and the customer service manager of the Springs, came around the corner. At six months pregnant, she still looked svelte and Beth never would have known she was pregnant if it weren't for the glow of happiness that surrounded the woman.

Beth certainly hadn't looked so radiant when she was expecting Jules. Of course, unlike Carmen, Beth had been barely eighteen, and totally alone. Not exactly the same situation.

"It is." Beth shook the snow from her coat. "And the roads are terrible. I'm lucky to be alive," she joked.

Carmen laughed and linked her arm into her friend's. "Well, I'm glad you made it." They started walking down the hall towards the staff room. "It's a big day today. Our first celebrity guest is checking in."

Beth's step faltered, and she hoped Carmen didn't notice.

She knew exactly who was checking in. To her irritation, she'd thought of little else since she'd heard the news a few months earlier. Slade Black. Beth forced a smile and tried her best to appear totally unaffected. "That's right," she said. "Sam was talking about that at the Grizzly Paw the other day." She felt like an idiot stating the obvious. Carmen had been sitting right there when her best friend, Sam, told them all that the lead guitar player for the band Jacked Crackers would be returning to their small town. Of course Sam had mentioned that news two months earlier, as well. Apparently he'd promised the band to stay until after Christmas. Not that Beth was paying attention. "He's that guitar player for the band Jacked Crackers, right?"

Carmen stopped and stared at her. "You know who he is. Didn't you meet him at the summer solstice festival?" Beth shrugged, feeling more and more like an idiot by the minute. "Maybe the cold is getting to your head." Carmen laughed and tugged at Beth's arm. "Let's get you warmed up with some coffee."

She couldn't agree more. It had to be the cold weather that was starting to affect her, because all she'd been able to think about for the past few days was the way Slade Black had looked at her when they'd met months earlier. There'd been more heat and promise of passion conveyed in that one brief moment than Beth had experienced in her entire life. Not that Slade would remember her. He probably looked at hundreds of women that way every day. And wasn't that what was really bothering her? That she was just another girl? "Coffee would be good," she muttered. She needed to shake Slade Black from her brain. She had no business lusting over a man. Particularly a rock star, with a reputation.

The sooner she could force him from her mind, the better.

SHE COULD ONLY GET through a few sips of her coffee before the gossip and chatter about Slade Black in the staff room started to drive her crazy. The Springs had only been open for little more than six months, so of course the news of their first celebrity guest was a big deal, but if Beth had to hear one more person squeal about how hot the guitar player was, or listen to the latest gossip about who he'd hooked up with on tour, she thought she might scream.

Besides, she had a full day ahead of her, so Beth mumbled a goodbye, grabbed her files and headed out towards the physiotherapy room. There might be a full-on winter storm raging outside, but her clients didn't have to worry about the treacherous roads or blowing snow as they were all guests at the Springs.

As she walked through the halls, Beth felt the same familiar sense of calm wash over her that she experienced every day. The entire resort had been designed with serenity and peace in mind, and the Harrison brothers, Trent and Dylan, had certainly accomplished their goal. Every detail had been considered, and she enjoyed just walking through the grand halls with walls made completely of glass: one showcasing the mountains just outside, the other highlighting the pools that made the Springs so special.

Each pool was filled with naturally occurring spring water that burbled out of the ground at a hot and therapeutic temperature. The water had long been thought to have healing properties, which was what brought people from all over the world to soak in their waters. And it was Beth's job to aid in that healing with as much physical therapy as her clients needed. For some, the water helped to rehab after surgeries, others were searching for cures to terminal illnesses, or more realistically, help making the transition. Then there were the guests who Beth never saw as a physical therapist. They were at the Springs for another type of healing.

She couldn't help wonder why Slade Black was checking in. Although something told her, it wasn't physical. Sam and her boyfriend, Trent Harrison, hadn't been very specific when they mentioned Slade would be visiting. But if it was physical, that meant it was only a matter of time before Slade, with his dark hair and even darker eyes, would be sitting on her table. She shook her head at the thought and refocused on the files in her hand as she walked into her therapy room.

She had no time to indulge in any of her ridiculous fantasies, anyway. Her first client, Mona Sheridan, according to the chart in her hands, would be there any minute. Beth had just enough time to turn on the lights and open the blinds, before changing her mind and closing them again because staring at a wall of white snow was not relaxing, and there was a knock on the door.

"Good morning." Beth opened the door for a woman whom, despite the pain in her eyes, wore a big smile. "You must be Mona." She extended her hand.

"I am." She shook Beth's hand. "I hope I'm not too early. I'm always early for things. It drives my granddaughter crazy." She followed Beth into the therapy room. "But I say, it's better to be early than late. No one needs to be waiting around for my ancient old butt to get moving and show up. Am I right?"

Beth laughed. "You're right and you're hardly ancient, and no, you're not too early. Just on time, I think." She gestured to the treatment bed, and noticing that Mona moved a little slow, moved a stool into position to help her up. "Let's talk about why you're here and how I can help you."

Mona took her time climbing up onto the bed and getting settled, but Beth didn't rush her. She also didn't move to help her, not because she was being insensitive, but because it was important to evaluate how mobile Mona was and what her limitations were. Her chart had mentioned increasing pain and decreased range of motion in the joints, but little else.

"Well, it's a good thing I was so early," Mona said when she got settled. "If it's going to take me that long to get up on the bed, I might need to start out even earlier next time."

"You're fine. We're not in a hurry." Beth's smile was warm. It was important for her clients to feel relaxed and at ease. After all, physical therapy was about getting better, or at the very least, relieving some pain and improving the condition. That went hand in hand with being comfortable. "Why don't you tell me your history and what brings you to the Springs?" Beth poised her pen over her chart, ready to take notes. "Then we can work together to get a treatment plan in place and get you feeling better."

"I have arthritis." Mona's words were so blunt and unexpected coming from the feisty woman that Beth's pen scratched across the page before she caught herself and looked up.

"Pardon me?"

"I have arthritis." There was no trace of self-pity in the woman's words. "I need you to help. I'm too young to feel so damn old."

Beth laughed. She was going to like Mona. "I will do my best to make your body feel as young as you feel on the inside, but I'm not a doctor, so when it comes to advanced arthritis, I can only do so much. There's no cure."

"I know that." The woman waved her hand and laughed. "But I keep hearing that the waters at the Springs are healing and I'm ready for some of that. I've had enough of treatments and diagnoses I don't want to hear. It's time to get better already. I need some of that miracle water."

Beth felt a flash of panic at Mona's words. She couldn't be sure if she believed in miracles or not, but she did know that she couldn't be held responsible for providing such a thing to a woman looking for a cure.

"Mona, I—"

"Before you object, just understand that I'm not looking for you to cure me. Just help." For the first time since she'd arrived, Beth saw the vulnerability in Mona's eyes. She really was a woman looking for hope. And maybe it wasn't a cure or a miracle, but hope was one thing Beth could do her best to offer and she could definitely help with alleviating some of her symptoms.

Her smile was shaky, but she looked Mona in the eyes. "I promise that I'll do everything within my power to help you feel your best, okay?" It might not have been much, but it was one promise Beth could keep and it satisfied Mona. And that's all Beth could really ask for.

The day flew by, with the morning filled with Mona, learning her history and starting her out with a therapy plan that included massage, soaking in the springs, and gentle exercises. It wasn't much, but given her diagnosis, there wasn't much more Beth could do. After a quick lunch, she saw two more clients and before she knew it, it was time to once again face the weather and head down to town to pick up Jules.

She'd done her best to avoid looking out the windows, or venturing far from her therapy room for most of the day, because it was easier to pretend the storm wasn't happening if she couldn't see it. The fact that Slade Black was likely somewhere in the resort by then didn't have anything to do with the fact that she was avoiding the main areas at all. Or at least, that's what she kept trying to tell herself. Not that it would matter if she ran into him anyway. He wouldn't remember her.

And what was to remember? They'd barely exchanged more than a few words, and that one searing look. But what had made an impact for her surely had barely been a blip on Slade's radar. It didn't matter anyway, she told herself as she gathered her things, and shut down the therapy room for the day. Even if by some off chance he did remember her, there was no way Beth could ever be interested in a guy like Slade Black. It's not as if she were a teenager anymore. It was all fine and good to daydream about celebrities and rock stars when you were young and had no ties, but as a single mother, she had a lot more to think about than her own desires. A lot more.

———

WHEN SLADE BLACK made the decision to leave his band, the Jacked Crackers, he hadn't really thought it through. Hell, like most things in his life, he acted first and would think about it later. The problem was, he thought as the SUV he was riding in rounded the mountain road, it was later. And he still hadn't thought about it. Maybe he could keep ignoring the entire situation, until it just went away. It was a strategy he'd used before with varying degrees of success. But something told him the continuous stream of phone calls and text messages from his manager were not going to be ignored. He'd have to answer them sooner or later. He owed his bandmates an explanation why he just couldn't handle one more day on tour. He just didn't have one, besides a lame excuse that he needed a break. He'd tried to leave months earlier, but the concert lineup was too intense; it was too big of a deal to leave his friends high and dry. So he'd waited until after Christmas, but day after day went by and it just got harder to leave. Until he just did it. Sure, the guys deserved a better reason than he gave them, he just couldn't figure out what to tell them. And he hadn't bothered to tell his manager, Max, a dammed thing.

"We're almost there," the driver told him. But Slade already knew that. He recognized the town of Cedar Springs, even though the quiet streets had been covered with a thick layer of snow since the last time he'd been there and he'd only actually been in the town for less than forty-eight hours, he would recognize it anywhere. It wasn't the bakery where he'd been treated to the most amazing cinnamon bun, or the local pub, the Grizzly Paw, where his band had played their gig at the summer solstice festival. No, it was an overwhelming sense of peace that washed over him just by being there that he recognized. Never in his life had he felt at home anywhere. Not since he was a little boy and his parents had still been alive. But that was a long time ago, and he'd almost not recognized the feeling at first. But for the last few months, no matter what luxury hotel the band stayed in, what exotic location they played, he couldn't fight the pull he felt to return to Cedar Springs.

"The roads are terrible, but I'll have you there soon." The driver tried again to make small talk, the way he had for the entire drive, but Slade just nodded, and offered him a smile. He wasn't trying to be rude, but he really needed to focus on himself and his thoughts for a little while. At least until he could figure out what the hell he was going to do next.

Fortunately, the SUV turned off, and was soon driving down the snow-covered lane that led to the Springs resort. Slade had only spent one night there, right in the middle of the opening craziness during the summer, but it was enough to know that the resort was definitely a place designed for peace and tranquility. They'd spared no expense as far as privacy and solitude was concerned. It would be the perfect place for Slade to figure things out. Which was good because he had no idea how he was going to answer his manager, Max Prior's, questions.

"Here we are." The SUV came to a stop, jarring Slade from his thoughts. He blinked and had to take a second look out the window. The Springs looked completely different than the last time he'd been there. Of course, that had been June and the blanket of snow that was currently covering everything had been absent.

Slade didn't wait for the driver to open the door. He

stepped outside, and immediately wished he hadn't. The wind whipped the snow off the mountains and blasted him in his face. He pulled the collar of his inadequate jacket up as far as he could and went to grab his guitar from the back. And just in time, too.

"Whoa." He easily reached over the other man and took his precious guitar, which was thankfully bundled in a travel case, out of his hand. "I got this." No way would anyone handle his guitar, except him. Ever.

The driver gave him a bit of a look, or maybe he didn't; it was hard to see anything with the snow stinging his eyes. "Go on inside, Mr. Black. I'll get the rest of your things."

The rest of his "things" was really just a large duffle bag, but Slade shrugged and, happy to get out of the freezing snow, hurried towards the door.

As he approached the building, and crossed over a low bridge that led to the front door, he was surprised to see the stream flowing beneath him was in fact, flowing. In the middle of January in the mountains, in what had to be sub-zero temperatures, there was no way the water should be flowing. But it was, the faint trace of steam wafting from it with under-water lights illuminating the stream in the dim wintry light.

A heated spring. Brilliant. Slade shook his head at the extravagance of it and hustled into the lobby as the doors slid open. Almost immediately, someone was there to relieve him of his wet jacket. He slipped out of it and immediately felt warmer, even in his simple, tight t-shirt. Despite the frigid outside temperature, it was warm enough inside, and Slade made a mental note not to leave again until spring.

As if he could hide that long. The thought hit him, but he shook it away. He'd give himself two days not to think of anything but resting. And then, he would answer the calls and try to make some sense out of his life. Two days wasn't too much to ask.

"Slade."

He turned to see Trent Harrison striding across the lobby towards him. He shook his outstretched hand when he got close enough and they shared a quick embrace with a slap on the shoulder.

"I'm glad you made it," Trent said.

"It is a bit sketchy out there. But I'm glad to be here."

"And we're glad to have you." Trent's smile was genuine, and Slade remembered the man's easy manner from the first time they'd met when the band played the festival. Trent was an old friend of Axel, the lead singer of Jacked Crackers, but it didn't seem to matter to either of them that Slade had called him last minute and told him he'd be coming to stay.

"It's good to be here, man." He shifted his guitar strap over his shoulder. "I hope it's not too—"

Trent cut him off and waved away any concerns before he could speak them. "The staff might be a bit curious." He tilted his head and Slade looked in that direction just in time to catch two Springs employees whisper and giggle to each other. Once they noticed they'd been caught, they quickly scurried away. "But I assure you that will die down. Your privacy and comfort is our priority. Anything you need, you ask."

Slade was used to asking for and getting anything he wanted at whatever hotel around the world he happened to be staying in. But he didn't want that here. He nodded and shrugged. "I don't want to be a bother."

Ignoring him, Trent put his hand on Slade's shoulder and guided him away from the registration desk and towards the great hall. "You're already registered," he said. "I have your keys and information right here and I'll take you up to your suite myself."

"You don't have to do that. Honestly, I'm good."

"It's not because you're a rock star." Trent grinned but

didn't stop walking. "It's because you're a friend. Seriously. Don't hesitate to ask for anything."

There was no point in arguing, even Slade could see that. So he resigned himself to his "special" status and enjoyed the view. The hall they walked down was completely glass on one side and showcased some of the many pools the Springs boasted. Slade remembered from his first visit that there were a few larger pools for soaking and even one large lap pool that was kept at a cooler temperature. But the majority of the hot spring pools were kept at a comfortable thirty-seven degrees, the same temperature that the water came out of the ground at.

Those pools were private and secluded, and guests could reserve them for their personal use. The waters were said to be therapeutic. But for what, Slade had no idea. Besides, he wasn't there for any type of therapy.

One of the many fountains caught his attention. "Hey. What's with the heated stream outside?" he asked, the question suddenly important. "Isn't that a little excessive, even for a luxury resort? I mean, it must cost a fortune to keep it flowing in this weather."

Trent started laughing and slapped Slade on the back. "Seriously, man. You know you're at the Springs?" He emphasized the last word, and as he did, realization washed over him.

"Oh no." He ran a hand through his too long black hair. "Of course. So you're saying, all the fountains and everything are filled with water from the hot springs?"

Trent nodded. "Every single one. It's all part of the ambience, you know?"

Slade shook his head, and his hair fell over his right eye, the way it always seemed to. "I must be more burnt-out than I thought. I'm not usually so damn slow."

"It's all good, man. All good. That's why you're here."

Indeed. Slade ran his hand through the burbling fountain

and let the warm water wash over his fingers for a moment. When he straightened, ready to follow Trent to the elevator bank and to his suite, his gaze landed on a flash of blond at the far end of the corridor. He'd taken out his contacts for traveling and because they kind of screwed with his rocker image, Slade hated wearing his glasses, so he couldn't see the face of the woman who stood there. And it was definitely a woman. His eyes weren't that bad. And he was well acquainted with the female form.

He squinted in an effort to make out the woman who, from the very little he could tell, simply stood at the other end of the room and watched him. It wasn't unusual. He was used to women watching him, but there was something about her. Even from a distance, and despite the fact that she was nothing more than a blur, Slade definitely wanted to know more. "Hey, Trent." Without looking away, he reached his arm out and tapped his buddy. "Who's that?"

"What? Who?" Trent turned and followed Slade's glance. "Oh, that's Beth. She must be done for the day. I'm surprised she's still…"

Slade didn't hear anything else Trent said. Instead, the name Beth repeated in his brain. Beth. Yes. He distinctly remembered meeting a very cute, very spicy blond named Beth last time he was in town. It hadn't gone much past the introductions and a brief conversation, but he remembered her.

Without thinking it through, Slade walked towards her and crossed the great hall so he could get a better look. Next time, he'd remember his glasses. Or more likely, his contacts. He'd only taken a few steps when Beth was gone. In a flash as fast as she'd appeared, she'd left. Unsure of what else to do, Slade stopped in his tracks. It wasn't as if he could go randomly walking around the resort to look for her. Well, he could. It was unlikely anyone would stop him. But he wouldn't.

"She must have had another client." Trent stood next to

him. "Or maybe she was on her way home." He gave Slade a strange look. "Do you know Beth?"

He shook his head. "No. Not really."

But it didn't mean he wouldn't. Suddenly, it wasn't the peace and quiet Slade looked forward to most.

It was seeing a certain blond again.

Chapter Two

WHAT HAD SHE BEEN THINKING? Standing there like a star-struck schoolgirl waiting to catch a glimpse of the sexy rocker? It's not as if she were sixteen anymore. She wasn't some googly-eyed teenage groupie who had any business even paying attention to a celebrity. Let alone a guitar player with a reputation.

Beth hurried to the staff room to gather her things. She was already running late, and her little star-sighting in the main hall didn't help matters. If she didn't get moving, she'd be really late to pick up Jules from school.

The staff room was almost empty, which Beth might have noticed as being unusual for that time of the day if she wasn't already totally distracted by the image of Slade in his tight black t-shirt, and equally dark hair falling over his eye, looking way too sexy than should be permitted at a resort known for its tranquility. Because the vibes he put off—hell, radiated—were far from tranquil. Really far.

"Where are you going?"

Beth, startled, turned to see Kurt, the head of maintenance at the Springs. With a cup of coffee in one hand, he lounged against a table. "Sorry." She took her jacket off the rack. "I didn't see you there. And, I'm going home." Beth stuffed her hands into her wool mittens, and did her best to bundle up against the weather that likely hadn't gotten any better. "I'm already running late." Her voice was muffled in her collar. "Hopefully the roads aren't too bad."

"They're closed." Kurt took a sip of his coffee and shrugged.

"Closed?" He had to be wrong. The roads wouldn't be closed because of a little snow. They lived in the mountains, for goodness' sake; they could handle snow. "Why would the roads be closed? What roads?"

Kurt pushed up from the wall and gestured to the coffee machine. Beth shook her head. She wasn't about to relax with a cup of coffee when she needed to figure out what was going on. Kurt must have picked up on her growing anxiety. "Sorry, Beth. I just found out myself. An avalanche covered the top few kilometers of the road. I'm sure they'll have it cleared by morning, but till—"

"Morning? I can't wait until morning. I have…Jules." She didn't wait for Kurt's response. Beth grabbed her purse, and still in her parka, ran to the lobby to find someone who could explain what was going on. She couldn't just stay at the Springs. She had a child to look after. And as much as Jules might think she was all grown up now that she'd had her twelfth birthday, there was no way Beth was going to leave her alone for the night.

"Dylan!" She caught sight of the general manager, who along with his girlfriend, Carmen and his brother, Trent, had become one of her good friends, and ran across the lobby to him. "What's going on?"

Dylan cocked his head and didn't even try to hide his grin. "Sorry," he said. "I can't understand a word you're saying."

With a frustrated yank, she pulled the zipper of her parka

down and pulled off her mittens. "What's going on?" she repeated. "Kurt said the roads were closed."

Dylan nodded. "They are. Sorry, Beth, but you're not going anywhere tonight. Not unless you can round up a sleigh and some huskies, but I wouldn't recommend it."

She glared at him, letting him know she didn't appreciate his humor. He'd see soon enough when his own child was born. Carmen was just six months pregnant, and it wouldn't take long for Dylan to realize how ferocious a parent's love could be. "I can't leave Jules." She turned and scanned the room for someone who might be able to take her down through the snow. "I'll find someone—"

"I'm sorry." Dylan put his hand on her shoulder. "I forgot about Jules." She shot him a look. "Why don't you call Samantha? Trent said she's stuck in town tonight. Maybe she could pick Jules up." She nodded, but continued to look for another alternative, despite the overwhelming evidence that there wasn't one to be found. "There's no way you're getting out of here tonight. Carmen will set you up with a room."

Dylan left her alone and, without any other alternative, Beth sighed and dug through her purse for her cell phone. After a quick call to her best friend Sam, who was indeed stuck down in town at her pub, the Grizzly Paw, and quite happy to hang out with Jules for the night, she tucked her phone away and went in search of Carmen and the hotel room she was promised. It might even be kind of nice to spend the night by herself. She couldn't remember the last time she'd had a night to herself, let alone in a posh hotel.

By the time she'd crossed the room and found Carmen stationed behind the registration desk, Beth had completely changed her mind about the snowstorm and the avalanche that had stranded her. She shrugged off her coat and draped it across the desk. "I hear you're the person to talk to if I want a room." She smiled at her friend, who only looked more and more beautiful with each passing day of her pregnancy. When Carmen and Dylan had first moved to Cedar Springs, from Castle Mountain Lodge, Beth wasn't sure if they'd all get along, but it hadn't taken long for them to all become close, and now Beth considered Carmen among one of her best girl-friends.

"I'm so sorry about the roads, Beth." So many years working in guest services had helped Carmen perfect her soothing voice designed to calm guests' anxieties in a crisis. "I have a room reserved for you and of course it's on the house. We're providing complimentary rooms for all staff who weren't able to get home in time."

Beth took the keycard. "Don't worry about me, Carmen. Now that I know Jules is going to be with Sam, I'm actually looking forward to this little break. I just can't seem to decide between ordering room service and eating in bed, or going down to Stillwater, the resort's in-house restaurant and soaking in the entire experience."

"Tough choice." Carmen grinned and leaned across the desk. "But selfishly, I vote for the restaurant. Dylan and Trent are supposed to have some sort of meeting tonight, so I'm on my own. We could have a girls' night and I'll get Jax to prepare us all the house specials."

Beth had only been lucky enough to try out the talented head chef's creations on one or two occasions, and the promise of house specials, coupled with a night catching up with her friend, made her decision for her. "Sounds perfect."

HE KNEW there was no point putting it off much longer. Slade dug out his cell phone and stared at the blank screen, trying to find the will to power it on. It hadn't taken long to get settled in his suite, which was far nicer than most of the rooms the band had been staying in, probably because of the reputation of rock stars trashing hotels—not that his band had done that. Well, not more than once or twice anyway. But that was a long time ago, when they were new and the shine of the rock and roll lifestyle hadn't worn off.

"What the hell," he muttered and pushed the power button. Within seconds, his phone lit up and chimed as message after message came through. Slade ignored them all and tapped in the numbers that would connect him to his manager, Max.

"What the hell, Slade."

"Hello to you, too." Slade was pretty sure humor wasn't going to help, but it's not as if he could do a lot more damage, so why not?

"Where are you?" Max ignored him. "You can't just take off as if nobody's depending on you. We have ten more cities to play and—"

"I'm taking a break." He looked out the window to the snow-covered mountains. The snow had stopped falling, but the scenery was now completely coated in a thick, untouched layer of snow that gave everything a very still feeling. He felt calmer just looking at it.

"You can't just take breaks whenever you want," Max said. Slade could imagine him in the hotel room in Philadelphia or Cleveland or wherever it was that they'd been last. He probably paced the room and smoked one of his ever-present cigarettes with no regard for the no-smoking rules that were most definitely in place. "The band is counting on you. You can't just leave. You're part of a group."

"Maybe that's the problem." Slade muttered the words before he could even think about what he'd said aloud.

But it was too late; Max heard them. "I'm going to pretend I didn't hear that, Slade. The Jacked Crackers made you, and if you think you can just take off without—"

"Enough, Max." Slade just needed him to stop talking. He'd always like his manager well enough, but at that moment if he had to hear one more word about how he owed everything to the band, and likely him, there was a very real chance that he'd say something he wouldn't be able to take back. "I got it. Besides, I didn't take off without a word. The guys knew, and I promised them I'd hang on until Christmas. It's January and—"

"You didn't tell me a dammed thing. Now tell me you're not leaving the band forever."

"Max, I'm—" Slade swallowed hard and walked to the large patio doors that opened onto a private balcony. Even though it was currently covered in snow and looking quite frosty, Slade didn't care. He slid open the door and let the arctic air blast inside. The frigid air felt good, reminded him of where he was and why he was there. He couldn't lie to Max. But he couldn't tell the truth either. Especially considering he had no idea what that truth was. "I need some time to figure things out."

"Slade, I—"

"I've been feeling the urge to write," he quickly interrupted his manager with the one thing he knew would shut him up. Max had been after him for months to write something new. *"You're only as good as your last hit."* He could practically hear his manager shouting his favorite catchphrase with a cigarette in one hand and a whiskey in the other. And since Slade wrote the hits for Jacked Crackers, the onus on that "last hit" fell squarely on Slade.

"You're writing again?"

"Not yet." There was no point lying about everything. "I just got here. But I will." Slade glanced at his guitar, still in its case. "I need some space for the words to come. I can't write on the road." It was true. Show after show in city after city, never mind the constant entourage that expected the band to live a rock star life, complete with partying every night, left no room for creative energy. Let alone a moment alone. Slade hadn't really planned to write when he decided to leave the tour; all he could think of was getting away. Being alone. Breathing. But if lying to his manager was what it took to buy him a little time, that's what he'd do.

"Where are you?"

Slade took a deep breath of the frosty air that started to numb him. The cold bit at his throat and almost made him cough with the intake of air. After a moment, he said, "I don't want to say. I need complete solitude to write."

"Slade, I don't–"

He heard the reluctance in Max's voice, which also meant he was unsure, so Slade took a chance. "Please, Max. I need this."

It was a risk. Slade had never asked Max for anything so serious before. Let alone using the word please. But this was important. More than important. It was crucial and something deep inside him told him if he didn't get this time, there would be no career to save.

Max must have known it, too. "Okay," he said after a painfully long wait. "I'll cancel some dates and do some shuffling. Two months. That's the best I can do. But after that, if you don't have a full album of hits…well…I don't know…"

If he'd been concentrating, he might have heard the threat in Max's words. But all Slade could focus on was the words "two months." It was longer than he'd imagined. Not that Max owned him. But he was their manager, and Slade knew it wasn't just his career he put in jeopardy. Axel, and the entire band, depended on him to not have a nervous breakdown and go totally off the rails.

"Did you hear me?"

Slade nodded, and then remembering he couldn't see him, said, "Got it. Two months." The wintry air still poured in through the door, and Slade could barely feel his fingers as he gripped the phone to his ear.

"I mean it, Black. Do whatever you have to do. But get me those songs and get back on this tour or—"

"I have to go."

He got what he wanted. A reprieve. Slade took the phone away from his ear, totally uninterested in whatever Max tried to threaten him with. He pressed the power button on his cell, turned it off completely and tossed it behind him on the bed.

"Two months." He repeated the words, still hardly believing how much time he'd just bought himself. Now all he had to do was figure out what the hell he wanted.

And while figuring that out might take two months, it certainly wasn't going to take that long to figure out that what he wanted at that moment was food. His stomach growled and reminded him it had been hours since he'd last eaten. The easiest choice was probably just to order room service and stay safely out of view from anyone who might potentially recognize him. At least for a day or two.

But the pull of room service and solitude wasn't enough to keep him safely out of the public eye. Not when there was a chance he'd see that gorgeous blond woman, Beth, again. He hadn't recognized her at first, but now that he knew it was the same woman he'd met months earlier at the solstice festival, he wasn't prepared to wait any longer than he had to for the chance to see her again.

***

EATING at Stillwater was always amazing. And definitely a perk to getting snowed-in at work, Beth thought as the waitress cleared their plates. The women denied the dessert menu, even though Beth knew it would be amazing. She couldn't eat another bite.

"I'm so glad you decided to join me. It's been forever since I've had a little girl chat and especially with…well, everything." Carmen dropped a hand to her expanding waistline. "It's nice to be able to just unwind with a girlfriend."

Beth smiled. "It is nice," she said, and meant it. "I can't remember the last time I've had a moment to myself, let alone just to sit and talk. Jules keeps me busy. I swear, some days I think the baby stage was so much easier and I wish for diapers and—oh, no, Carmen." Beth rushed to cover her words when she noticed the look of panic on her friend's face. "It's not that it's all terrible or anything. It's just that…"

"It's hard," Carmen said. "I know. I can't imagine how you do it on your own, Beth." Neither could she half the time, Beth thought but didn't say. "But Jules is a great kid. Whatever it is you're doing, you have to teach me. If my baby turns out half as awesome as your daughter, I'll be happy."

Complimenting her on her parenting skills was a surefire way to make Beth blush and she looked down at the table with a shrug. "Thank you. Jules is a great kid. I know I'm very lucky."

"It's not luck. It's you." Beth looked up to see Carmen staring at her very seriously. "I mean it, Beth," she continued. "It can't be easy raising her on your own and with everything kids have to deal with these days."

Beth took a swallow of her wine. "Don't even get me started." She wasn't about to scare Carmen with stories about cyberbullying at school, and Internet safety concerns, let alone all the rest of the things twelve-year-old girls had to deal with. Carmen would figure all those things out on her own when the time came. "But I wouldn't change it." Beth smiled because it was the truth. Despite everything. Having Jules on her own, the challenges, the sacrifices. She wouldn't change a thing. "I love Jules and our life together. We have everything."

Carmen's smile was warm, but she raised an eyebrow. "Everything?"

Beth knew exactly what her friend was getting at, but she wasn't about to discuss her dating life, or lack thereof. It was incredibly depressing to talk about something that didn't seem to ever change. Especially when all around her her friends were paired up in these impossibly happy couples. Even Rhys, her one-time high school sweetheart, had found his true love. For a while after Beth moved back to Cedar Springs, she'd entertained the idea of rekindling things between them, but they both knew it was farfetched and after Kari Fox came to town and stole Rhys' heart, that window was closed for good.

In an incredibly lame attempt to change the subject, Beth said, "So have you thought about a baby shower yet?"

"Samantha wants to have one." Carmen waved her hand. "Don't change the subject. When are you going to start dating? You can't be alone forever."

"I'm not alone."

"You know what I mean."

Beth took another swallow of her wine and swirled the remainder of the liquid around in her glass. She'd need more wine if they were going to talk about her sex life, or lack thereof. And it was pretty clear that Carmen was adamant about going there. "I do know what you mean."

"But?"

"There's no but." Beth tried one more time to put off her friend, but when Carmen raised her eyebrow and tilted her head in disbelief, Beth gave in. "Okay fine. It's not that I don't want to date, it's that there's no one *to* date. It's not like this town is bursting with eligible men." Carmen opened her mouth but Beth cut her off before she could say anything. "Single men." Once again Carmen opened her mouth. "Under the age of seventy-five," Beth said sharply. "Preferably younger."

Her friend didn't even attempt to stifle her laugh. "Okay, I see your point. It's not like Cedar Springs is crawling with young, single eligible men. But there has to be at least one."

Beth looked down at her napkin, not wanting Carmen to see the heat that spread across her features because there in fact was at least one man who had caught her attention and he was most definitely in Cedar Springs. In fact, he was in the very building she was in. Single? Yes. Young? Yes. Hell, sexy, strong, and incredibly gorgeous? Yes. But eligible? Definitely not.

"Oh, I know that look."

She reached for her wine glass and downed the last swallow. "There's no look." She shook her head but didn't meet Carmen's eyes.

"Who is he?"

"It doesn't matter." And it didn't. She was probably just imagining the ridiculous connection she felt with Slade and even if she wasn't, it didn't matter. He was a rock star and a guest at the resort. It's not as if there was a future with a guy like that. There was no point pursuing anything. "It's silly anyway."

Carmen narrowed her eyes. "I doubt very much that it doesn't matter. And I'm going to get it out of you if it's the last thing I do. But first," she pushed up from her seat, "I have to visit the little girl's room. I swear this kid is lying right on top of my bladder."

Carmen excused herself and left Beth alone to give her a minute to pull herself together. She couldn't tell her friend about whatever it was she felt for Slade. Especially when she didn't even know him. Ten minutes of chatting and flirting, months ago, was definitely not enough for even a crush. She must be losing her mind. She reached for her wine glass.

Empty.

BY THE TIME the elevator came and Slade made his way down to the restaurant, he didn't care what they were serving: he was prepared to order one of everything.

"Good evening, sir." The hostess who greeted him was professional and friendly. And if she recognized Slade at all, she didn't give any indication. He smiled, instantly put at ease. Maybe the dining room wouldn't be such a bad idea after all. And hadn't Trent told him the staff would be discreet? "Will anyone be joining you this evening?"

Slade shook his head. "Table for one, darlin'."

The girl smiled and picked up a menu. "Absolutely. If you'll follow me, sir. We have the best table in the house."

A quick look around the restaurant told him that pretty much any table would be the best in the house, but he didn't bother to say anything. Instead, he nodded and followed the pretty girl through the dining room. He only made it about halfway when the sound of laughter caught his attention. He froze. Something about the sound captured him. It was beautiful, and so…free. When was the last time he'd laughed?

He ignored the hostess and turned in the direction of the sound.

Her.

Beth.

He stood and watched her, undetected for a moment. She was with a friend, and even with her back to him, Slade could see that she was enjoying herself. He wouldn't interrupt.

"Excuse me, sir." The hostess tapped him lightly on his arm; her fingers lingered a little longer than was necessary. Reluctantly, Slade tore his gaze away from Beth and her friend. "Your table…" She lowered her eyes seductively and Slade knew if he wanted to, he'd be able to take the beautiful girl back to his room later. He knew because it was an all-too-familiar scenario. It was also one he'd lost interest in long ago.

He kept his smile neutral and nodded, while he subtly slid away from her touch. "Right. Sounds good." Before he turned, he saw Beth's friend get up from their table and excuse herself.

"One moment," he said to the hostess. "There's been a change of plans." Before she could protest, he took the menu from her hands with a smile and moved quickly through the tables, right as Beth reached for an empty wine glass.

"Looks like you could use a refill."

BETH SPUN at the voice and found herself staring directly at a black t-shirt that covered what was obviously a very hard, chiseled stomach. She swallowed hard and was instantly annoyed at her body's response to the man in front of her. Slowly, she looked up, hoping to use the extra seconds to regain some semblance of control over herself.

"I'm good," she said. "Thanks."

The second she made eye contact with Slade Black, she regretted it. Not because she didn't like looking into those dark, deep eyes, but because she did. Too much.

"I didn't ask you how you were doing, sweetheart." His grin was slow and easy. The look of a man who knew exactly what effect he had on women. "But I'm glad to hear you're doing well. Now, how about that drink?"

She should have been offended at his forwardness. She should have told him exactly where he could take his bold assumptions right before she stood up to leave. Instead, she laughed.

It was the kind of laugh that started low and quiet, and ended up in almost a snorting sound. Her hand flew up to her face. Had she seriously just snorted? If she could have done it with even a modicum of grace, Beth would have crawled under the table and disappeared right then. But she couldn't, so she did the next best thing. She smiled and said, "Actually, I think I do need another glass."

Her mother had always told her to fake it till she made it. And although Beth was pretty sure she wasn't referring to a situation quite like the one she found herself in, it seemed like a pretty good solution to the mortifying situation she seemed determined to build for herself.

Although, the moment Slade sat down across from her, Beth instantly rethought her strategy. She couldn't sit across from this man and have a conversation with him as if he were some normal guy. He was anything but normal. And even if he was, she didn't know how to have a conversation with any guy who was even remotely normal, and not either engaged or dating one of her closest friends. The truth was, Beth was sadly out of practice with men.

The waitress materialized at their table almost before Slade had pulled out the chair. No doubt all the servers had been huddled in the back, watching and silently praying that he'd sit in their section. Beth watched while he ordered her another glass of wine and a whiskey for himself. She used the slight reprieve to pull together her thoughts. It wasn't the fact that Slade was a rock star that had her insides all twisted, although that didn't help. But it was something else that made her uneasy. Something she didn't want to think about.

When finally the waitress left, and he turned to face her, Beth knew exactly what it was that made her stomach flip. It was the way he held her gaze completely and left no room to look away. His dark eyes mesmerized her and it was clear that Slade Black knew exactly what type of effect he had on women. And was having on her. She had to put a stop to it.

She forced herself to look away. Beth pulled her cell phone

out of her purse and quickly checked it to see whether Jules had called.

"Am I keeping you from something?" His smooth, deep voice washed over her and she looked up to see his sexy grin.

With a sigh, she put her phone down. "No. I'm expecting a call from…" She hesitated to say Jules' name. It was hard to date with a child; usually as soon as the guy heard she had a kid, they were out of there. And it wasn't as if she wanted to date Slade—she shut down the little voice in the back of her head that disagreed—but it would be kind of fun to pretend, even for a minute, that she could if she wanted to.

"Not a husband, I hope."

She shook her head and had to bite back a laugh. "No. I'm not married."

Right then the waitress returned with their drinks and Beth took a deep drink. She needed to focus and get control over herself.

"Trent thought maybe you were on your way home," Slade said, surprising her. Sure, she'd seen him earlier in the corridor, but surely he didn't notice her, or pay any attention. "When you disappeared so quickly, I mean." He took a swallow of his whiskey.

If she didn't know better, she might think that Slade was nervous. Beth almost giggled at the thought that the gorgeous, confident rock star in front of her might be nervous to talk to her. It gave her confidence. "You were asking about me?" She tilted her head and smiled while she waited for his answer.

It took Slade a moment, but when he put his drink down, all his attention was focused on her, any trace of uncertainty gone. "I did."

Two simple words, but they pierced her with their direct-ness and the intensity behind them.

She swallowed hard. She might lack experience, but even she

could see he was interested in her. Not that it would ever happen. With the lifestyle he must lead, Beth wasn't about to fool herself that she was more than a passing interest, but even if that's all it was—especially if that's all it was, she mentally corrected herself—there was no way it was going to happen. She was a mom and way too responsible to let herself go there. She was not some groupie. The knowledge freed her, and in an odd way, gave her power.

She ran her finger along the edge of her wine glass, and slowly licked her lips before she asked, "And what did you learn?"

"Not nearly enough."

"And what is it you'd like to know?" To her surprise, once she'd relaxed a little, she fell easily into flirting. Maybe she wasn't as rusty as she thought she was.

"I'm sorry, am I interrupting?"

Beth jumped at Carmen's voice and sat back in her chair. Guilt flooded through her, which was ridiculous because she hadn't done anything wrong. Except totally ditch her. "Carmen, I'm so—"

"It's fine." Carmen's smile was genuine as she turned to her companion, who had immediately jumped out of his seat to greet her. Points for being a gentleman. "And you must be Slade. I'm Carmen Kincaid, the manager of guest relations. Trent told me you'd be coming. We're happy to have you."

"Thank you." He extended his hand, which Carmen took. "I couldn't be more pleased to be here. I'm assuming I hijacked your dinner date."

Despite the fact that he acknowledged his intrusion, Beth couldn't help but notice that he didn't say anything about excusing himself.

"You did," Carmen said. "But that's fine. I think I'm going to take this pregnant body to bed. Dylan and Trent should be almost finished with their meeting anyhow."

"Carmen, you don't have to go." Even as she said it, Beth

knew there was no way Carmen would intrude on what she no doubt thought was a very interesting situation. She was pretty sure she'd be interrogated later anyway for any details.

"Honestly, I'm exhausted. But I'll catch up with you tomorrow, okay?" Beth didn't miss her friend's wink before she turned and left them alone again.

HE WAITED UNTIL CARMEN LEFT, and gave Beth a moment to compose herself. For a moment, he thought she would follow her friend out and leave him alone, but to his surprise, she'd stayed. She'd been full of surprises. From the cute way she'd accidentally snorted when she laughed, to the steadfast way she refused to be swayed by his charms. Maybe he was out of practice, but Beth didn't seem to be falling for any of his usual moves.

It was refreshing. And more than a little intriguing.

"I hope I didn't interrupt something there. But when I saw you sitting alone, I thought to myself, 'now there's a woman who should never be alone,' so you see, I just had to come sit with you."

She tipped her head back and the laughter that came from her was sweet and sexy, second only to the creamy length of her exposed neck.

"That's smooth." She sat up and took a sip of her wine; her tongue darted out to lick a stray drop from her lip. The move made him happy to be sitting down. "And no, you didn't interrupt anything. In fact, I was just getting ready to turn in for the night."

"You still have wine to drink." He leaned back and crossed one leg over the other, doing his best to look relaxed when he felt anything but calm. "If I can't convince you to join me for dinner, at least finish your drink."

"I already ate."

"Dessert then." When she didn't immediately say no, he took it as a good sign and added, "Besides that, it's too early to go to bed. Especially when you have such good company to enjoy the evening."

Her smile lit up her face. He couldn't remember the last time he'd seen a sight so beautiful. She reached back to smooth her ponytail and pulled it over her shoulder where she fidgeted with it. "It sounds enticing, but—"

"It's okay to say yes." He wasn't going to let her say no. There'd been something about her when he'd met her in the summer, something he hadn't been able to get out of his head. And now that he sat across from her, he knew it hadn't all been in his head. There was no way he was going to let her get away so easily. "Unless you have to get home."

The moment the words left his lips, Beth flinched and pulled back. "I'm not going home tonight."

Slade knew he could take those words and twist them into a thousand dirty scenarios starring the two of them upstairs in that very plush looking bed. He also knew that Beth wasn't that kind of woman, and by the look on her face, even if she was that type of woman, that was definitely not what she meant.

He pulled himself together enough to continue the conversation. "If you aren't going home, then where are you going?"

"I'm staying here."

Whatever he'd expected her to say, that wasn't it.

"Have you looked outside?" She raised her arm and pointed across the restaurant to the picture window that looked out over the gardens. Or what would be the gardens if they weren't completely blanketed in snow. Slade took his time following the length of her arm with his eyes, greedily drinking in the sight of her bare skin where her t-shirt ended, down to her slender wrist with what looked to be a twist of string wrapped around it. "There's a major blizzard going on." She dropped her arm and caught him staring at her. "Or didn't you notice?"

"Oh, I noticed. But I just assumed that you all knew how to drive in snow."

"We all?" Beth crossed her arms over her chest, which had the benefit of pressing her breasts up and together so they strained against the cotton of her shirt. Slade made a mental note to make her angry again.

"You know what I mean."

"Yes. I do. And we do." She dropped her arms. "But not when there's an avalanche. Not even I can get through that, so here I am. Stranded."

"I'm not going to pretend that I'm not happy about it." Slade leaned forward slightly with a need to close the gap between them. He knew he was coming on strong with her, but he couldn't seem to stop himself. And what was even more frustrating was that she seemed totally unaffected by his charms. Any other woman would have crawled across the table into his lap by now.

But Beth wasn't just any other woman. And wasn't that exactly what was drawing her to him.

"Stay." The word came out low and deep. "Just for dessert."

"I don't—"

"You have time since you don't have to rush home." He caught her eyes and stared into their clear blue depths. "Let me guess, you're more of a cheesecake girl than chocolate, am I right?"

Her smile told him he was right. "Well…"

Taking a chance, Slade slid his hand across the table and rested it over her slender fingers. She would agree; he knew she would. She just needed a bit more convincing. He slid his fingers under hers, so he held her hand in his. "What would it hurt?"

She didn't pull her hand away and when Beth opened her mouth—to consent, Slade assumed—he didn't bother hiding the grin that spread across his face, despite the fact that he knew it was very uncool and if any of his bandmates had seen it, he'd never hear the end of it.

But the grin was short-lived when a popular, and somewhat cheesy song, broke the silence between them. In a flash, Beth pulled her hand from his grasp and flew to her cell phone on the edge of the table.

"Sorry. I didn't pick the—" She flipped it over and looked at it. "I have to take this." Her eyes met his as she stood, and Slade could see the cloudy conflict in them.

Slade jumped from his seat, his hand out to stop her. "I'll order you—"

"No. I have to go."

There was no way he was going to let her slip away that easily. Not the most interesting, surprising, and very sexy woman he'd had the chance to meet in years. It wasn't going to happen. She was already a few tables away when he called out her name. When she turned, he said, "I'll see you again. That's a promise."

Chapter Three

THE NEXT DAY, the crews had cleared the road and Beth managed to get herself out of the resort and down from the mountain in time to check on Jules before school was meant to start. As it turned out, the town had closed the school because the roads weren't safe enough for the buses to drive on. Which meant Jules got a snow day and because she didn't want to risk getting trapped up the mountain again, Beth took a personal day. At least, that's the excuse she gave Carmen when she called in.

And her friend, being the understanding person she was, totally bought it. But she did ask about Slade, and even though Beth tried to keep her answers as neutral as possible, she knew it wouldn't be enough.

"I'll fill you in when there's something to fill you in on, okay?"

"Come on, Beth. I'm in a boring old relationship now. I need to live vicariously through you."

"A boring, old relationship? Wow. You make it seem so appealing." Beth rolled her eyes and quickly took a peek in the pantry. Maybe her and Jules could do some baking? When was the last time she'd had time to do that?

"You know what I mean," Carmen said. "And you and I both know that it's not every day that you have dinner with a rock star."

"I had dinner with you." She stifled her laugh.

"You're infuriating."

"I know I am. But I have to go. Enjoy your weekend. I don't work again until Monday and with this snow, I don't think we'll be going anywhere."

She could hear Carmen's heavy sigh on the other end of the line. "Okay. But make no mistake, I will be asking you again."

"Oh, I wouldn't make that mistake." Beth shook her head and peered into the living room, where Jules was huddled on the couch and watched one of the stupid tween shows Beth hated, where the characters were all over-the-top and ridiculous. "I'll see you Monday." She hung up the phone before Carmen could keep prying. Beth knew Carmen wouldn't let it go until she told her something about Slade. The thing was, there was nothing to tell. Unless she mentioned the way he could undo her completely with just one look, or the way his touch had burned her skin but made her yearn for more at the same time.

No, she couldn't tell anyone those things, because she didn't understand them herself. She didn't understand anything about the way she felt about Slade. Except she needed to let it go. There was no way she was going to get involved with a rock star guitar player. Especially one with a reputation for being a ladies' man. That was the last thing she needed in her life. She looked in again on Jules, who tried so hard to be grown up and act tough, when really she was stuck between being a woman and a child. Twelve was a hard age. And to think, she was only a few years older when she herself had become a mother.

Beth forced the thought from her head. No. She wasn't going to go there. She'd grown up way too fast. There was no harm letting Jules be a kid as long as possible. Even if it meant silly shows. She left the phone on the kitchen counter, went to join her daughter on the couch and slid in next to her.

"Hey, is there room for me on here?"

Without waiting for an answer, Beth squeezed onto the couch next to Jules, tucked her legs under the quilt and pulled her daughter in close. Without tearing her eyes away from the screen, Jules rested her head on her mom's shoulder in silent acceptance.

When the show was over, Beth flicked off the television. "I thought since we're snowed in, we might as well make the best of it. What would you say to some baking?"

Jules twisted around and stared at her mother. "What do you mean by baking?"

"I mean flour, sugar, old aprons, and the smell of fresh cookies and cinnamon buns in the house. What do you say?"

"I say you're crazy." The look of teenage indifference that Jules was starting to perfect settled onto her face. "We don't bake. Grandma bakes."

Beth wasn't going to give up so easily. It wasn't often the two of them were given such an opportunity to hang out together. She did not want to waste it with one or both of them stuck in front of a screen. "It doesn't mean we can't. Come on, it won't hurt to try."

For a moment, it looked as if Jules was going to reject her offer. And it wouldn't have surprised Beth if she had, but for as much as Jules grew up and pulled away, she also liked to be yanked back every once in a while. "Okay." She tried to hide her smile. "But we for sure get to try cinnamon buns."

"PAIN IS the sound your heart makes…" Slade sang the words while he strummed the strings of his guitar. In disgust, he grabbed the sheet of paper in front of him and crunched it in a ball before he tossed it towards the trash can. He missed. Just like half the others he'd thrown in that direction. "That's terrible." He pulled his guitar off his neck and propped it up against the chair. "Pain isn't a sound." He stormed across the room and stared out at the snowy mountains.

He'd been trying all night to write something. Anything. After Beth left him at the restaurant, he'd been unable to sleep. She'd preoccupied his every thought, which was ridiculous. She was just a woman. A woman who hadn't fallen for his smooth lines and every other move that usually worked to get what he wanted. Which, in this case, was definitely Beth.

Maybe instead of trying to write a song about heartbreak, he should be writing one about trying to get the girl? It wasn't something he'd ever tried before. Slade almost laughed aloud at the idea. It also wasn't something he'd ever had trouble with before.

He ran his hands through his hair and tugged in an effort to relive the pressure that built inside him. Maybe that was the point? Maybe instead of writing the same old "I've got a broken heart" power ballad, it was time to try something different?

The band would hate it. But what else was new? They'd pretty much hated everything Slade'd done, or more to the point, not done, for the last few months. Axel and the rest of the guys were trying desperately to hold on to something that wasn't there any longer. They weren't the same band they were five years ago. Fame had changed them. At least some of them.

Five years ago, when he'd walked into that smoky bar and stepped up on the stage for open mic night to perform his song, "Cards Up My Sleeve," he had no idea how his life would change. Of course, like any singer-songwriter, he'd been hoping to be discovered, but Slade never could have guessed that Axel, a young musician trying to get his band off the ground, would be sitting in the audience that night. He liked Slade's sound, they decided to partner up, and soon after, the band took off. The years in between had been a blur of concerts, hotel rooms, recording studios, parties, and women.

He was done.

The pressure in Slade's head built as he paced around the suite and relived the memory. He needed to get out. As nice as the room was, spending almost twenty-four hours staring at the same walls with no one else to talk to would make him crazy.

He took his guitar with him and headed down to the main hall of the resort. People milled about—a few obviously recognized him and he happily signed a few autographs—but for the most part, he wasn't bothered. He didn't know where he was headed until he found himself in front of the physiotherapy room. He hesitated, but only for a second before he walked through the door.

A man behind the desk looked up when he walked in. "Do you have an—" He broke off as recognition crossed his face. "Slade Black, right?"

Slade nodded. "The one and only." He glanced around the small waiting room. "I'm looking for Beth. Beth..." He hesitated, as he realized he didn't even know the last name of the woman who wouldn't get out of his head.

"Beth Martin?"

Slade took a chance and nodded.

"She's the only Beth who works here." The man looked down at a computer screen. "Do you have an appointment? I didn't see anything—"

"No. I was just..." What was he doing? "She said something about some exercises for my fingers." Thinking up the lame excuse on the spot, he held up his guitar. "So they wouldn't cramp when I was playing." If the other man hadn't been watching him strangely, Slade would have smacked himself for thinking up such a stupid reason for coming to see her.

"Of course," the man said. "I bet you get a lot of strain with all the playing you do. And after a while, if you're not careful, it might develop into a bigger condition, like carpal tunnel or tendonitis. You're smart to get it looked at, especially in your line of work. If you jeopardize your—"

"Yeah, well...is she here?"

"Beth? No."

Slade swallowed down his growing impatience.

"She's off till Monday. But I can show you some exercises if you like?"

"No." He shook his head and turned to leave. "I'm good." He left before Beth's co-worker could say anything else and he resumed his wandering.

He hadn't realized how much he'd been looking forward to seeing her again. It was a feeling he was totally unfamiliar with and dammit if it didn't eat him up inside. He found a quiet corner with a white leather chair placed next to a large fountain and without hesitation, pulled his guitar to his lap and started playing.

The rhythm started slow but after a few minutes of playing with different chords, he settled into the sound. When he opened his mouth, the words started to flow, and he went with it, for the first time in a long time, singing from the heart.

"When you walked in, there was no one else,
Blond hair swinging,
blue eyes staring into my heart,
Baby, making you love me is just the start."

He smiled while he played and let the music take over. He fidgeted over different words, tried different things until finally, he had it. He sang it through a few more times and then, as if in a daze, he put his guitar aside and looked up. A woman, who looked to be in her sixties, sat on a couch a few feet away and knit. When he stopped playing, she looked up from her project.

"Well, don't stop on my account. That was just lovely."

Despite years of practice, accepting compliments on his work wasn't easy. Particularly new projects. "It's just something I'm playing around with."

"Well, I like it." Her needles moved together again. "For whatever an old lady's opinion is worth, anyway."

He laughed. "It's worth a lot, actually. Thank you. But I'm afraid I'm going to forget it all if I don't write it down soon. You wouldn't happen to have any paper, would you?"

She put her knitting down and reached into her bag before she produced a piece of paper. "It's not ideal." She started to struggle to her feet, but Slade jumped up, crossed the space between them and allowed her to sit back in her seat. "Sorry, I'm not as nimble as I used to be. I'm Mona."

"Simon," he said, spontaneously deciding to use his given name. He took her offered hand, flipped it and dropped a chaste kiss on it. "It's a pleasure to meet you."

"Well, aren't you quite the smooth operator?" She grinned, but he could see the pain on her face. "It's not every day I have a man both serenade me and kiss me on the hand. It certainly is a pleasure, Simon…"

"Just Simon."

"Oh, it's never 'just' anything, young man. Besides that, I have the feeling that you are definitely more than a 'just.' Much more."

He couldn't remember the last time a woman had made him blush, particularly a woman old enough to be his mother. But Mona had done that in the first thirty seconds of meeting her. He took the paper she offered him and flipped it over. It was a knitting pattern.

"Are you sure you don't need this?" He tried to hand it back but she shook her head. "It looks important."

"Don't need it. I've been doing this for a long time. There's nothing that piece of paper can tell me that I don't already know."

He looked at her skeptically. But from the look of her knitting, she did seem to know what she was doing. Not that Slade would be able to tell. He had very limited experience with knitting, or anything that wasn't store bought, really. There hadn't been a lot of handicrafts, or even home cooked meals for that matter, in his childhood. And he did need some paper.

"If you're sure?"

"I'm sure, Simon." She picked up her knitting again, and the sound of needles clacking together filled the space between them. It was an oddly comforting sound, almost rhythmic. "Besides, if you're going to use it to write down those beautiful lyrics you were just singing, well, I'd be honored."

Slade nodded. "Yes ma'am." He walked back to his chair and his guitar, but she stopped him.

"She's a lucky girl."

He didn't bother to pretend there was no girl. He turned, the smile splitting his face. "She is. Now I just need her to realize that."

SLADE SPENT the rest of the weekend working on the song, and the start of another. It was the most he'd written in months. And it was so different from anything he'd written, too. There was no question, he'd been productive holed up in the Springs but by Sunday afternoon, he was more than ready to get out and change the scenery. Lucky for him, he'd managed to talk Trent into lending him his car, with the promise that he wouldn't drive it off the road, wrap it around a tree, or leave it in town. They were easy promises to keep, or at least that's what he'd thought before he started out on the icy mountain roads. He grew up in Toronto, and as a city boy he'd never had to worry about driving in such conditions.

With white knuckles, and a speed he was sure his grandmother would probably laugh at, he inched his way down the mountain and into the town of Cedar Springs. He hadn't been in town since summer, and even then it was only for a few days. Just long enough to play the gig and fall in love with the town. And maybe, that wasn't all he'd fallen in love with. The thought popped into his head unbidden and he almost immediately pushed it out. It was not only ridiculous to think like that, it was also not possible. He didn't love. Never had, and he couldn't see that changing anytime soon.

It wasn't until he got to Main Street and had the car safely parked did he realize he didn't actually have anywhere to go in town. He'd been so worried about getting some fresh air, and getting out of the hotel, that he hadn't bothered to think much beyond that.

It was the first time in a long time Slade didn't have his schedule packed with interviews, gigs, appearances, studio time, or any other number of things jammed into his day. He laughed at the freedom of it, and got out of the car and walked.

Despite the shining sun, the air had a bite to it and he pulled his leather jacket tight around him. He wished he owned something a little warmer, even if his stylist didn't approve.

He didn't bother trying to hide his identity under a baseball cap like his bandmates and the only reason he wore dark aviator glasses was to shield his eyes from the sun glaring off the snow that seemed to completely cover the town. There was no doubt that everyone in town already knew he was there but despite a few people who asked him for autographs, which he signed happily, he was largely left alone. He wandered and looked in store windows until the smell of fresh baked cinnamon buns stopped him in his tracks.

How could he have forgotten? The best damned cinnamon bun he'd ever had.

The smell filled his senses. Slade turned and headed straight across the street to Dream Puffs. He couldn't take another step until he had one of those cinnamon buns in his hand. And maybe a cup of steaming coffee to go with it. After all, he still hadn't had more than a couple hours of sleep in the last few days. But at least it wasn't because of a girl, but because he'd been up writing about that girl.

He couldn't figure out which was worse.

"Good afternoon." The lady behind the counter greeted him with a smile and flicker of recognition in her eyes. "What can I get you today?"

"Darlin', when I was here a few months ago, you served me the best dammed cinnamon bun I'd ever had or had the pleasure to have since."

"I remember. I'm Suzy, by the way." She winked. "And I'm very good with faces."

Slade laughed. "Well then, I don't mind telling you that your cinnamon bun is the reason I just had to come back to your lovely town." It wasn't entirely a lie. "I've been dreaming day and night about them. I might even have to write a song about them. That's how passionately I feel."

Suzy put her hand to her chest, and her friendly smile turned into a frown. "After a passionate endorsement like that, I'd like nothing more than to give you one."

"Why do I get the feeling there's a 'but' coming?"

The baker clenched her teeth and gave him a nod full of regret. "I just sold the last one. Well, actually, I sold all of them just a minute ago."

"All of them?" He narrowed his eyes and when she pointed past him, over Slade's shoulder, his eyes followed and landed on a young girl who held a box of what had to be *his* cinnamon buns.

"All of them." Slade turned and grinned at Suzy.

"What are my chances here, you think?"

"A famous guitar player and a twelve-year-old girl?" Suzy laughed. "I'd say pretty good."

Slade accepted the coffee she offered him and with a nod of his head, turned to direct all his charms on a girl he hoped was a fan. He ignored the looks he got from the other patrons as he made his way across the small shop.

"Excuse me. I have to ask you a very important question."

The girl turned and with very suspicious eyes—familiar eyes—she looked up at him. Likely she'd been taught never to talk to strangers. But there was a flicker of familiarity in her gaze, too. He could work with that.

When she didn't say anything, Slade took it as a good sign and continued. "Would there be any way I could convince you to give me one of those cinnamon buns? It's a matter of life or death."

"Whose death?"

"Mine. If I don't finish the song I'm working on, my manager will kill me."

The girl tried, unsuccessfully, not to smile. "A song for the Jacked Crackers? That's pretty important, I guess."

"You know who I am?" Slade knew damn well that she knew who he was. It wasn't often that he wasn't recognized. Especially by anyone under the age of forty.

"Everyone does." She shrugged. "But I still don't understand what a cinnamon bun has to do with a song?" Her head snapped up.

"I can't explain it, but I was busy working on a song and then, bam, I got a craving for one of these cinnamon buns. I won't be able to write another word without one."

The girl swallowed a laugh. "You're not writing songs

about baking, are you? Because I would totally listen to that song. My mom made me bake this weekend even though we both suck at it. I don't think there was one thing we could eat." She held up the box.

"That would explain why you bought the whole box of buns, then?"

"Yup. She promised me cinnamon buns. This seemed like the best option." She smiled and once again, Slade had the distinct impression that he'd met her before. "I'm Jules, by the way."

"Nice to meet you, Jules. I'm Slade."

"I told you. I know who you are." She shook her head slightly and put the box down on a nearby table. "The kids at school are going to freak out when they hear about this, you know?" She opened the box and offered him a cinnamon bun.

"You're not freaking out?" And she wasn't. In his experience, young girls were the craziest fans. It wasn't unusual for them to scream when they saw him, or start crying. Or both. Jules didn't do either of those things. It was refreshing. She seemed like a cool kid, plus she gave him one of his cinnamon buns, which meant she was definitely a cool kid.

He took a bun and nodded his thanks.

"You're just a guy," she said with an indifferent shrug. "Like a super famous guy, but still." She closed the box and picked it up again. "I should probably go. My mom's going to wonder where I am."

"Thanks for this." He raised the half-eaten bun. "You've totally saved my song. I think I'll be able to write again."

She laughed. "Glad I could help."

Slade walked with her to the door. "I should get going too, but I don't really have anywhere to go. Mind if I walk with you?"

"Sure." They fell into step on the sidewalk and Slade crammed the rest of the delicious bun in his mouth. It was every bit as good as he'd remembered it. "It's no wonder you don't have anywhere to go," Jules said. "There's pretty much nothing to do in this town. Why'd you come here? You could go anywhere. Cedar Springs is lame."

"I don't think it's lame. It's quiet."

"Quiet's lame."

Slade smiled. "Sometimes quiet is exactly what you need."

BETH WATCHED while her best friend, Samantha, worked behind the bar. The Grizzly Paw was closed on Sundays but that didn't stop Sam from cleaning and puttering all day. The woman rarely took a day off, which was a large part of the reason she'd managed to save her father's business from complete ruin and turn things around when she took over operations of the pub. Despite some of the struggles, the Grizzly Paw had become a destination in the town of Cedar Springs. It was certainly a destination for Beth, who loved the opportunity, no matter how rare, to catch up with her friend.

"Thanks again for hanging out with Jules the other night. Mom's not back from Phoenix for another two months, which means my options are pretty limited."

"No problem." Sam waved her hand and pointed to the coffee maker. Beth nodded despite the fact that Sam's coffee was notorious for being unbearably strong. "I'm glad it worked out." Sam poured the coffee. "I couldn't get back up to the Springs anyway. Besides, you know I love Jules. It was fun."

Sam had moved up the mountain to live with Trent at the Springs in the fall. Despite the fact that she still spent most of her time at the pub, Trent needed to be close to the resort and they needed to be close to each other, so it was an arrangement that worked for them. Unless, of course, there was an avalanche that closed the road.

"What did you do with your night to yourself, anyway? Carmen said something about the two of you going for dinner."

Beth looked down and focused intently on a paper beer coaster. No doubt that wasn't all Carmen had told Sam. Word traveled fast in a small town, particularly among friends. Friends who were always trying to set her up. "We had a nice dinner," she said vaguely. Beth knew without looking up that Sam was likely staring at her with one hand on her hip, waiting for the details. After a few seconds of silence, she looked up.

"And?"

"And it was great. Jax is a fabulous chef and the food is always—"

"Cut it out." Sam threw the rag she'd been holding. Beth caught it easily and smiled innocently. "Tell me about Slade."

"Carmen has a big mouth."

"You know you'd tell me anyway." Sam snatched the rag from Beth's hand and polished glasses. "So talk. I knew there was something between the two of you at the festival last summer. And now he's back. What do you think it means?"

"I think what it means is that he's here for a vacation and happens to be staying at the same place where I work so we ran into each other. That's what it means." Beth did her best to seem nonchalant and unaffected, but the truth was all weekend she'd been trying to figure out what it might mean. If it meant anything at all.

"You and I both know it means more than that." Sam shot her a look and Beth stuck out her tongue. "I'm going to pretend I didn't see that. Now, tell me about the other night. What did you talk about? Are you going to see him again? How long's he here?"

Beth laughed and took a sip of her coffee. She grimaced and pushed it away. There was no amount of sugar or cream that could fix that. "Just a few questions, huh?" She shook her head. "It doesn't matter anyway, because I'm not seeing him again. Not that I *saw* him or anything. It wasn't like it was a date." She could feel the blush heating her face. "You know what I mean. But I'm not seeing him again."

"I know what you mean. And I think you're being ridiculous. Why wouldn't you see him again? He's obviously interested in you."

"No he's not." She protested, but it was a lie. She may be out of practice with men, but she knew enough to know that Slade was interested in her. Either that or she totally and completely misread the way he looked at her with so much heat in his eyes that he could melt a glacier. Or the way his touch had burned her fingers and sent sparks all the way through her to a place she'd long thought gone. There was something between them, that much she was certain of. But connection or not, it couldn't happen. She was also certain of that.

"I'm not going to argue with you about it." Sam shot her a look. "Because you and I both know you're lying. But why won't you see him again? What's the harm?"

What was the harm? Beth spun the coaster around on the polished wood slab and tried to pull her thoughts together. She'd tried to distract herself all weekend by hanging out with Jules, but she couldn't stop the thoughts of Slade—the way he looked in his black t-shirt, the smooth way he'd convinced her to have a drink with him, the look in his eyes when he stared at her, and pretty much every single detail about him—that relentlessly pushed themselves into her mind. The reality was, there was a lot of harm that could come from seeing Slade. Sam couldn't understand; she didn't have a daughter to think about.

"Don't worry about Jules." Beth jerked upright and stared at her friend, who'd just read her mind. "It's not like you have to marry him, Beth. But you're allowed to have a little fun. And a hot guitar player—it doesn't get more fun than that. Am I right?"

"It's not that simple, Sam."

"Seems like it to me." Sam jumped up, sat on the counter behind the bar, and swung her legs as she spoke. "He told me to lighten up and have a little fun, remember?"

"I remember."

"Look at how well that advice worked out for me, Beth. You never know what could happen if you don't try. Besides, worst-case scenario, you get to fool around with a rock star god once or twice and in my mind, that is not a worst-case scenario."

Beth didn't even try to hide her laughter and she wasn't even going to pretend that the idea of fooling around with Slade wasn't appealing. Hell, it was a whole lot more than appealing and she'd be lying if she said the thought hadn't crossed her mind once or twice—or pretty much totally occupied it for the last forty-eight hours—but there was no way she was going to admit that out loud. Particularly not to Sam.

Especially not to Sam. She didn't understand that it wasn't that simple. It couldn't be that simple. There was Jules. And even if her best friend didn't seem to think that it would matter to have a casual fling, she didn't have a daughter to think about. Let alone an almost teenage daughter, who was a lot more aware of things than anyone gave her credit for. No. Beth needed to set an example, not entertain thoughts of sexy rock gods.

"No, Sam. It's not happening." She shook her head. "The best thing for everyone is for me to get him out of my head totally."

"Who?"

Both women spun around to see Jules, who held a large box from Dream Puffs, with Slade next to her. If she could have, Beth would have disappeared into the floorboards.

"Who are you getting out of your head?" Jules asked again. She walked across the room and put the box down on the bar. "Mom, Auntie Sam, this is Slade." She waved vaguely in the direction of Slade, who'd followed her in. He looked at Beth in question as he heard the introduction. Maybe she wouldn't have to worry about getting him out of her head after all. Now that he knew she was the mother of a twelve-year-old, he probably wouldn't bother with her again. It seemed to be the trend with most men.

"We've met," Beth said after a second.

"Oh yeah. At the concert, right?" Jules hopped up on the counter next to Sam. "I forgot about that. So you kinda already know everyone then?"

Slade nodded but didn't take his eyes of Beth. "I do. But I'd definitely like to get to know all of you better."

A shiver traveled across her skin and settled in her core when he spoke. Maybe she'd been wrong and he wouldn't be put off by the fact that she had a kid. The idea did something to her insides that reminded her of being a teenager again.

"Especially now that I know Beth's the mother of the girl who saved my life," Slade added casually.

"Pardon me?" She stared at them, but Jules just started laughing. Evidently, Slade had the power to turn even her own jaded pre-teen into a giggling schoolgirl. "What happened? Are you all okay?"

"I am now." Slade's face lost all traces of his usual humor and he nodded grimly. "But it was a pretty dire situation for a while."

"What happened?" Sam looked just as concerned as Beth felt.

Jules and Slade looked at each other. Slade waved his hand towards her, and Jules nodded. "Basically, Slade's trying to write some new songs."

"Am writing new songs," he corrected.

"Whatever." Jules shook her head. "So he's writing songs, and if he doesn't get them done, his manager is going to kill him."

"Jules," Beth interjected. "I hardly think his manager is going to kill him if he—"

"No." Jules raised her voice. "He will. It's serious."

Beth looked to Slade, who nodded solemnly. "It's true."

She shook her head. "So how exactly did you save his life?"

"I gave him a cinnamon bun."

Sam burst out laughing and jumped off the bar. Beth shot her a look and turned back to her daughter. "A cinnamon bun?"

"I hope you don't mind, but—"

"I don't care." She waved away Jules' protests. "But how did that save his life?"

Slade took a step closer to where Beth sat. He locked eyes with her, and instantly her stomach flipped. His heady scent, a mixture of sugary sweet and crisp outdoor air, filled her senses and made it next to impossible to focus. "I'm afraid that was my fault," he said, his voice low. "I may have told your daughter that I wouldn't be able to finish the song I was writing if I didn't get a cinnamon bun."

"And his manager would kill him."

"It's true." Slade nodded solemnly. "See? She saved me. Your daughter is a hero."

Jules giggled. Beth shook her head but not before she smiled along with them. It had been awhile since she'd seen her daughter so relaxed and happy. The moodiness of a pre-teen was not easy to deal with, but in only a few minutes, Slade seemed to have broken through. Not that she should be surprised.

"Well, I'm glad she could be so helpful for you." Beth pushed out of her seat. "But we should get going and Sam's not even open today, so I'm sure she had things to do."

"Nope." Sam lounged against the counter, a sly smile on her face.

"Well, we do have stuff to do." She looked at Jules, who no longer smiled and was back to her usual hormonal sulking. "Like homework," Beth said pointedly. "It was nice to see you again, Slade." She tried to slide past him, but when he didn't step back, her chest brushed his, and despite the thick sweater she had on and the leather jacket he wore, her body reacted instantly to his touch.

WHEN SHE TOUCHED HIM, sparks flew through his body, and it was all he could do not to grab her, pull her close, and press his lips on hers for the kiss he'd wanted to take almost from the moment he'd met her.

"Excuse me." Beth muttered the words, and it was just enough for Slade to break out of the trance she held him in and step back to let her pass.

"Sorry." He didn't take his eyes off hers, and he knew enough about women to see the heat in her eyes, too. She seemed hellbent on denying it, but Slade knew he had an effect on her. "It's too bad you have to run off." He worked to keep his voice casual, but with Beth it wasn't easy to maintain the easy facade he'd developed over the years.

"Mom, do we have to go right now?"

Slade started at the use of the word Mom. He'd definitely been taken off guard to discover that Beth, as young and beautiful as she was, was a mother of an almost teenager. With any other woman, he would have already run as fast as he could in the other direction if he'd found out they had a kid. But Beth wasn't a regular woman and not surprisingly, her daughter wasn't a usual kid.

"Let me buy you dinner." The words flew out of his mouth

so quickly, he didn't even have time to think about what he asked, or why, or who else was in the room until Beth and Jules answered at the same time.

"No, I—"

"For sure."

He could see she struggled to maintain her composure as she glared at her daughter. "No." It was only a small word, but everyone in the room could see Beth meant business. It didn't mean he was going to give up, though.

"As a thank-you," he said. "For the cinnamon bun. I don't think you realize how big a deal it really was."

Beth shrugged into her puffy black coat and reached behind her to pull her long, blond hair out. She let it cascade down her back, completely unaware of how gorgeous she was. "I'm sure a cinnamon bun is a very big deal in your world where you get whatever you want, whenever you want it, but here in Cedar Springs, it's just called being friendly. Dinner really isn't necessary." Her words stung, which Slade was sure they were meant to do. She'd pushed him away from the beginning, but if there was one thing Slade enjoyed, it was a challenge and that's exactly what Beth was.

"Regardless, I'd like to say thank you." He stared directly at her and pinned her with his dark eyes.

"Yeah, Mom. Let him say thank you." Neither of them looked away, locked as they were in their stare-off. He would not look away first, but he dared her to with a wink.

"You have school in the morning, Jules."

"School's important." Slade saw an opportunity and took it. "Perhaps another time? Next weekend? So it won't interfere with school."

He'd backed her into a corner and there was no way she could say no. They both knew it. Beth swallowed hard. Her blue eyes blazed; she knew she'd been beaten. With a grin, he looked away, letting her have one small victory.

"That's a great idea," Sam contributed and Slade made a mental note to thank her for being on his side. "Next weekend is the skate party—you could all go together."

"Skate party?"

"It's really cool," Sam continued. "There's a big bonfire on the ice, and some different food booths set up. The whole town comes out. It's a lot of fun."

Slade looked to Jules, who shrugged with indifference. "Sounds good," he said. "You can both be my dates?" That made Jules giggle and Beth sigh.

"Do you have skates?" Beth said. "Because it's a skating party, so if you don't have—"

"I'll get some."

Beth sighed again, and zipped up her coat. "I'm sure you will. Come on, Jules."

He watched as they walked to the door, and right before she slipped out, he called, "I'll see you this week to work out the details, Beth."

"You don't have my number." He noticed she didn't make any move to give him her number, but it didn't matter.

"Not to worry. I'll find you."

She shook her head and with a blast of cool air as the door opened, she was gone. Slade waited a minute, and turned to Sam. "Thanks for backing me up."

She picked up her rag and polished the counter. "Hey, my girl needs to have some fun. But just so you and I are on the same page—" She stopped what she was doing and pinned him with her eyes. "I know all about your lifestyle and your bad boy reputation. If you hurt her or screw with her heart in any way…"

He raised his hands in surrender. "I'm not that guy anymore. And I promise you I won't do anything to hurt her." There were a million things he could say to try to convince her that he wasn't the guy that the tabloids portrayed. He hadn't been that guy for a long time. But there was no point; Sam would form her own opinion, and either way it didn't matter.

He said his goodbye to her and left the pub. The only thing that mattered was getting Beth to see that he wasn't some rock and roll bad guy. And the only way he was going to do that was by getting close enough for her to see it for herself.

As he walked down the street, back to where he'd parked Trent's car, Slade's head filled with words, and the start of a new song.

Chapter Four

MONDAY MORNING, Beth was running late getting to work. She'd slept past her alarm, which never happened. But it also never happened that she had sexy dreams about rock stars with black leather jackets and muscular arms that held her close, driving her dream self to distraction with his kisses. She hadn't even realized how late it was until Jules, who thankfully woke herself up, came into her room to check on her. She'd hopped out of bed, with what she hoped wasn't too much of a guilty blush on her skin, and straight into a shower.

If she hadn't already been so late, she might have even entertained the idea of relieving the ache between her legs that her dream had left her with. All the way up the mountain to the Springs, she'd tried to push it out of her mind. It was ridiculous. She couldn't remember the last time she'd had such a dream, particularly with someone who was not and never would be her lover. The whole thing was crazy. He was getting into her head, and she needed to put a stop to it.

Whatever it was that Slade Black thought he was doing by harassing her, it needed to stop. He may be used to getting exactly who and what he wanted, but it wouldn't be her. No, it couldn't be her. She was a responsible mother of a twelve-year-old girl; she didn't have time to mess around with a guy like Slade. Especially one with a reputation like his.

It didn't seem to matter how much justifying she did in her head; even as she hustled down the corridors on her way to the therapy room, she couldn't stop her eyes from checking out the guests to see if Slade was one of them.

"Good morning." Josh, her co-worker, greeted her with a wide smile the second she walked through the door. "You'll never guess who was in here looking for you on the weekend?"

She could guess, but she wasn't about to tell Josh that. He lived for gossip, and judging by the amount of tabloid magazines he read, he likely knew more about Slade than she did. Which, admittedly, wasn't all that much. "Who?" She did her best to pretend she had no idea what he was going to say.

"Slade Black." Josh slapped his hand down on the counter. "He said you'd offered to give him some exercises for his wrists."

"Did he?" She picked up the stack of files for the clients she'd be seeing and flipped through them.

"He did. And he would only see you." Josh sounded as if he'd been changed profoundly by his close encounter with a celebrity, which, judging by how excited he was, maybe he had. "I hope he comes back. Maybe you could ask him to sign something for me? I'll bring in my iPod. Do you think he'd—"

"I'm sure he would." Beth gave him a placating smile. "I'll let you know if he comes back. But I really should get to work." The second she turned away, Beth shook her head in wonder. She'd had no idea Josh was so star-struck. It would probably drive him over the edge completely if he knew the truth.

Her first client was Mona, and Beth couldn't think of a better way to start her morning. In the very short time she'd gotten to know the woman, she'd really come to like her. She knocked slightly before she opened the door to the treatment room. The second she walked in and saw the pain on the woman's face, Beth's smile vanished.

"Good morning, Mona." She tried to keep her voice light. "It's good to see you. How was your first weekend at the Springs?" She gestured for the woman to lie back on the table, which she did with only a small flinch of pain.

"It was lovely," Mona said. "It's absolutely beautiful here, and I think just being at the Springs is making me feel better."

Beth smiled, and gently started bending first one of Mona's legs, and then the other. She'd reviewed the woman's chart and contacted her doctor. Mona had advanced arthritis, and the best course of treatment that Beth could offer would be to keep her mobility up and her pain controlled as much as possible. "It is pretty amazing here. Have you had a chance to get into the pools yet? I think it will really help you to soak in the spring waters, and there are some exercises I can show you to do while you're in the water that will really enhance treatment."

Mona shook her head. "I'll be honest. I've been too busy enjoying just looking out the windows. All the snow is beautiful and is so relaxing." Beth finished with one leg, and moved on to the next. She was pretty certain that if Mona had to deal with the slippery snowy roads, she might change her mind about the beauty of the white stuff. "I know you think I'm crazy, but there's something about a world blanketed in snow that calms the mind."

"I'll take your word for it." Beth laughed. She liked Mona. She had a good spirit, and Beth could imagine if it weren't for the arthritis crippling her, she'd be an active, vibrant woman.

"And the people I've met here," Mona continued. "So interesting. And talented."

"Talented?" Beth began a light massage on the woman's foot, and gently rotated the ankle as she did so. "I know my

massages are good, but I've never been called talented before."
She smiled when Mona laughed.

"You are good, my dear, but I was referring to the young
man who serenaded me the other day." Beth froze momentarily. Slade. It head to be him. "He was writing a song about a
woman and by the sounds of it, she's a very lucky woman."

I'm sure she is, Beth thought to herself. No doubt, Slade
was writing about one of his groupies, or that generic
"woman" that most musicians sang about. The elusive, beautiful, sweet and oh so perfect woman who dominated almost
every song in the charts. If one such woman actually existed,
she'd be surprised, let alone enough of them to provide the
inspiration for so many songs. She shook her head. As far as
Beth was concerned, Slade and all the rest of the musicians out
there were perpetuating lies about love with their fictional
characters.

"You don't believe me?" Mona pulled back and stared
at her.

"I didn't say that." She tried her best to neutralize her face,
and continued with the mobility massage. "I'm sure there's a
very lucky woman out there somewhere who's the star of many
songs."

Mona shook her head and clucked her tongue. "You're far
too young to be so jaded, Beth. Love exists, and I think you'd
be surprised to discover it's actually not that hard to obtain."

"I didn't say it didn't exist. I just have a hard time believing
that the idealized women these songs are written about exist.
And I think it's impossible for the average woman to achieve
the kind of love that's sung about in songs or written about in
books. It's just a big—"

"Don't say it." Mona held up a finger. "Don't burst my
bubble about love songs." She smiled, and Beth couldn't help
but smile along with her. "I'm still holding out for my Prince
Charming. My Charlie was special, but he's been gone a long

time now." Mona dropped her head back on the pillow. A sigh escaped her as Beth's fingers moved up past her ankle. "There's a lot of love to be had in this world, my dear. But if you don't believe, it'll pass you by and you won't even realize it."

Beth stopped her massage and grabbed an ice pack from the cooler they kept on the counter. "I guess I just think that if it can so easily pass me by, maybe it's not worth having in the first place." The words coming out of her mouth shocked her. Did she really believe that love was a ball she had to catch in the air or miss forever? And what if it wasn't love she was looking for anyway? She tucked a towel around the pack and placed it over Mona's ankles. "I'm going to let you sit for a few minutes and then we're going to head down to the pools so I can show you those exercises I was telling you about."

Mona ignored her, intent on her conversation. "Are you trying to tell me you've never been in love before?"

Beth thought about it for a moment before she answered. "I honestly don't know. I think I thought I was in love with Jules' father, but now, looking back, that was definitely not love. But that was a long time ago. I haven't really dated much, to be honest."

"A pretty girl like you? I don't believe it."

"Believe it. I've been kind of busy with my career and raising a daughter. At the end of the day, there's not a lot of time for romance, even if it did come along. Besides that, I don't think I'd recognize it even if I did fall in love."

Mona sighed and shifted on the table. "You sound like my Bria. Except for the granddaughter part." Mona laughed. "She's so serious, always working on some new project, or assignment. She's a photographer, you know."

Beth nodded. "You told me."

"And she's very good at it, too." Beth could hear the pride in Mona's voice. And also the annoyance as she said, "But she's not getting any younger, and she refuses to believe that she can have both a career and a relationship."

"Kids these days." Beth laughed and picked up the chart to scribble a few notes.

"It's true. You kids are wasting so much time when all you really have to do is open yourself up to the possibility that you can have it all."

"Even if I wanted it all, Mona," Beth paused and tapped the end of the pen against her lips before continuing, "I'm so far gone that I'm afraid I wouldn't even know I was in love until it was too late."

Mona propped herself up on one elbow and looked at Beth with a glint in her eyes. "Well, maybe that's exactly what should happen then."

SLADE HAD BEEN at the Springs for almost a week, and still hadn't been in the actual spring water. It was a situation he planned to remedy as soon as he finished one more verse. He'd been up almost all night after he ran into Beth and Jules in town; his brain had been totally preoccupied with both of them. As he'd navigated Trent's car back up the icy mountain road, the idea for a new song had formed in his mind, and as soon as he had his guitar in his hand, the words had come easily.

There was no doubt, Beth was his muse. If he believed in muses, which he never had before. But he'd never had a Beth before. And even if she pushed him away, there was no doubt that she fueled his creative fire. Along with other fires. Whatever it was, he needed to get closer to her.

And then there was Jules. Halfway through the night, he realized that Beth's daughter needed a song of her own. Sure, he'd had plenty of teenage girl fans in his career, but he'd never met a kid as interesting and cool as Jules. Plus, he thought with a smile, she'd given him a cinnamon bun. If that didn't deserve an entire song, he didn't know what did.

Fueled primarily on coffee and French fries he'd had the kitchen send up, Slade was more than ready to get out of his room and stretch his limbs a bit by the time he wrote the last word. It was definitely a rough draft of what he knew would be a hit. But it was a start and that's all he needed. Riding his creative high, he quickly changed into his swim trunks and headed down to the pools.

From what Trent had told him, there were two pool areas: The private soaking pools could be reserved for exclusive soaking with guaranteed privacy. Or the general pools, in the main room, which was much less private, but also had what he wanted. A swimming pool. And that's exactly where he headed. He swiped his key card and greeted the attendant who handed him a towel.

"Good afternoon, Mr. Black. Would you like a private pool today?"

He shook his head. "Not unless I can do laps in it, sweetheart."

The girl giggled, the way most girls did when he was around. "I'm afraid not." She pointed to the windows behind her. "You'll find the swimming pool in the main spring room. Just follow the path; you can't miss it. We also have a variety of other temperatures if you'd like to experience the healing powers of the natural springs water, and for an exhilarating experience, try the plunge pool. It's kept at a cool temperature of twenty-five degrees."

"Sounds a bit less exhilarating and a little more frosty to me."

The girl leaned in and spoke in a husky voice. "It'll make you feel alive."

Slade nodded and took a step back from the counter. He

was pretty sure that wasn't all the girl was implying that would make him feel alive, but neither option seemed all that enticing to him at the moment. "I'll keep that in mind."

She stood up and flashed him a bright smile. "Let me know if you need anything else, Mr. Black. I'd love to help you out."

Oh, I'm sure you would, he thought as he made his escape and headed through the change room area and out into the main spring room.

The air was hot and thick with humidity, a stark and welcome contrast to the icy world outside. Slade could feel his muscles warming as he walked through the room. He took in the plants and waterfalls that fell into a stream that seemed to wind its way through the entire room. The entire effect was created so well, Slade could feel the tension melt away before he even set foot in the pool.

After he passed a few larger hot tubs, with signs telling him what temperature the water was and the benefits of soaking, he arrived at the large lap pool. Without hesitation, he dropped his towel on a nearby lounge chair, kicked off his sandals and dove in. The water slid over his body as he kicked under the surface. He stayed under as long as he could, and released bubbles of air slowly, until finally his lungs ached with the need for oxygen. He broke the surface; he pulled one strong arm out and let it arc gracefully before it cut through the water again.

Lap after lap, Slade churned the water, letting his body fall into line with the exercise. Swimming had been his one constant no matter where he went. Once the Jacked Crackers started making some money, they always stayed in hotels that had a pool; he'd made sure of it. Because when life got crazy, which it always did when he was on the road, at least he could lose himself in the peaceful monotony of swimming.

With only a few others enjoying the lap pool, Slade had the luxury of an entire lane to himself as he let his mind clear of everything as he focused on his strokes. Finally, when he started to feel the familiar fatigue in his arms, he slowed his pace and came to the tiled edge. He wiped the water from his eyes, and slicked back his hair before he rolled his shoulders, and let the tension slide away.

He didn't bother counting laps, or keeping track of how long he swam. It depended on the day, and how much stress he had to let go of. He hung out at the edge of the pool for a moment to let his heart rate return to normal. As soon as it did, he started to feel the coolness of the water and hauled himself out, in search of a hotter tub to soak in for a bit.

Slade didn't have to look for long to find the pool he wanted to use. He picked up his towel and had hardly taken two steps when a familiar flash of blond hair caught his attention. He homed in on Beth instantly and even with a dozen other spring pools to choose from, there was nothing that could stop him from joining the one she was in.

It wasn't until he got closer that he noticed she was with someone else. "Mona," he said casually as he shed his towel and slipped into the warm water. "It's nice to see you again."

The older woman lit up and grinned. "And you, Simon." He didn't miss the look Beth shot him when she heard the use of his given name. "I want you to meet my physiotherapist, Beth."

Given the excuse to stare at her in her bathing suit, he turned towards her and he couldn't have kept the smile from his face if he'd tried, and he hadn't. Her blond hair was pulled up in a high ponytail, and she wore a simple blue one-piece, with The Springs embroidered over the chest. Slade let his eyes linger over the embroidery as he took in her uniform. "We've met." He didn't take his eyes off her.

The effect she had on him was becoming a problem. Particularly considering he completely lost sense of himself whenever he was within five feet of her.

"Yes." Beth spun and created a swirl of water around her.

"We've met." She didn't sound very happy with him, but that was hardly an unusual state. "And if you don't mind, I'm with a client."

Slade watched while she turned her back to him, and tried to resume her session with Mona. But his new friend was obviously very astute, and was clearly on his side. "Don't be silly, Beth," she said. "We were almost done and besides that, I think you've given me enough to work on. You don't want to fill up this old head of mine with too much information. How will I keep it all straight?"

"Mona, we still have ten minutes, and—"

"And you said yourself that I should soak in one of the hotter pools for that time." She made her way to the stairs, and Slade helped her as she made her way, shakily up and out of the pool. "And if you don't mind, I think I'd like to be alone to absorb everything we discussed today." She winked at Slade, so only he could see, and before Beth could protest further, she picked up her robe and left.

He turned and faced Beth, effectively blocking the steps, and her escape, as he did so.

"EXCUSE ME." Beth tried to control her breath and her annoyance. She wasn't being very successful on either front.

Slade took a step down the steps. Water droplets slid down his chiseled abs and disappeared into the waistband of his swim trunks. Beth swallowed hard and hoped he didn't notice. "I'm sure you don't have to run off right away." His voice was low and rough, and combined with the way he looked at her, Beth didn't know whether she should run away or take another step closer to him.

"I have clients." Her excuse sounded thin, even to her own ears, and she could hear the shake in her voice. "I need to go."

He crossed his strong arms over his chest and took another step to close the distance between them. He was near enough now to touch, and Beth knew she should just take a step back, but she couldn't. He held her mesmerized with his dark eyes. "I think you have a few minutes."

"That's presumptuous." She tried to control the waver in her voice.

"No." He reached out to smooth back a stray hair from her face. "I was paying attention. You don't have another client for at least ten minutes." He was close. Too close. Beth struggled to control her breathing. What was it with this man that made her lose her senses? "Just give me a minute," he whispered, his words a breath on her lips. "Just one."

She licked her lips, and it was only when she saw the look in Slade's eyes that she realized the effect it might have had on him. A shiver of power and…something else went through her at the idea. "Okay," she said before she realized what she'd agreed to. "Just one."

The corners of Slade's lips curled up into a smile and he stepped the rest of the way back into the hot water. The bubbles and froth swirled around their bodies, and Beth had to drag her eyes away from the way the water danced against Slade's skin. His body was perfect. Everything about his chiseled, bare, and smooth chest was what she would expect from a rock star god, or at least a man who considered himself one. He even had two tattoos. One was a chain of musical notes wrapped around his bulging biceps, but another, larger one of a guitar traveled up his rib cage, peeking just out of his waistband and ending just under his arm.

She wanted to reach out and touch it, to turn him just enough so she could see the end of it. Where it wrapped around his ribs onto his back. Instead, she squeezed her hands together under the water and willed herself to have some control over herself.

"Do I scare you?" He asked the question as he took another step towards her and closed what little space there was left between them.

She shook her head slightly. "No." The word came out firm and certain, and for a moment Beth thought she might once again have her emotions reined in. But then she added, "How you make me feel scares me." The second the words were out, she bit her lip. Had she seriously just said that?

"I don't want to scare you." He reached out again. This time, instead of tucking a piece of hair back, his finger trailed along her cheekbone. "I'm so incredibly drawn to you, Beth. I can't explain it." She closed her eyes against his touch. A small, insufficient defense mechanism against the heat of him.

It was too much. His closeness, the heat of the water, his words, his everything. She forced herself to take a step back, but he clasped her arm in his hand. "Don't go."

Beth shook her head. "I'm not going anywhere." And she wasn't. But she did need space. She couldn't think with him so close. Not when she could smell his musk, his scent that was just all man and sex and rock and roll.

She squeezed her eyes shut and ran her wet hands over her ponytail. Water droplets trailed down her shoulders. How could one man be so intense? It was too much. Just being close to him, with that way he looked at her and his touch on her bare skin. She needed to gain control. Some perspective. She only felt how she felt because he was the first man in years to give her any attention. But that wasn't true and she knew it. Plenty of other men had flirted with her over the years. She'd even dated a few. No one had ever come close to setting her nerves on fire with just a single touch the way Slade did. Not even close.

"Go out with me."

"Pardon?"

"Go on a date with me." He leaned in, hovered over her

and once again closed the gap between them. "A real date. Let me buy you dinner and—"

"I already agreed to go to the skating party with you on Friday." Her chest heaved; her voice came out in small puffs as she spoke. "What more do you want from me?"

Slade's lips turned up in a wicked grin. "Such a good question." He moved smoothly through the water, his steps slow but sure, as he backed Beth up against the tile wall. She didn't once break eye contact with him, and when he lowered his head, so she could practically taste his words, he added, "I want so much more from you than simply skating."

If she was the prey, he'd successfully stalked her and she was completely at his mercy. Beth couldn't be sure whether it was the temperature of the water or Slade's proximity, but she was definitely overheating, and her senses had completely abandoned her. She licked her lips again, this time, totally aware of how he would look at her with so much heat and hunger in his eyes. "Slade, I—"

"Beth."

In an instant, Slade jumped back and a rush of cool air hit Beth in the face as she felt his absence. She took a deep breath and quickly looked up to see Kari Fox, her co-worker and now friend, staring down at her. There was a sly smile on Kari's face as if she'd realized a moment too late that she'd interrupted something. "Kari." Beth struggled for composure. "What's up?"

Kari flicked a knowing glance to Slade, who'd retreated to the other side of the small pool before she continued. "Dylan sent me to find you. He said something about a staff meeting later. He wanted all the department heads there."

Beth struggled to focus on what her friend said, which was next to impossible with Slade staring at her from across the water with that look in his eye, and every nerve ending in her body yearning for his touch again. She needed to get away from him. It wasn't healthy. She needed space and distance. Whatever it was she felt wasn't appropriate. Not for a single mother, not for the workplace, not for...any of it.

"Tell Dylan I'll be there. I assume he left details in our mailboxes?"

Kari nodded. "I'm sorry if I interrupt—"

"It's fine." Avoiding the stairs completely so she wouldn't have to go past Slade, Beth lifted herself out of the pool. "And you didn't. I was just getting out. I have another client."

"You didn't answer my question." His voice was thick, and Beth purposely kept her back to him so she wouldn't be lured in by his sexy eyes.

"I think I answered it enough."

Kari shot her a look and raised her eyebrows. Perfect. Now she'd go tell her boyfriend, and Beth's good friend, Rhys, that there was something going on with her and Slade when there really was nothing going on. Or, was there? More importantly, did she want there to be something?

"I'll see you later, okay, Beth?"

Beth whirled around to tell her that no, she'd go with her now, but Kari raised her eyebrows at her and tipped her head in such an obvious way that Beth swallowed her frustrations. "Fine." She pushed the word out through gritted teeth. Kari disappeared so quickly, that even if Beth was going to use her for escape, the opportunity was gone.

She wrapped a towel around her body, eager to hide herself from the eyes that still burned into her skin. It was insane the way he affected her with one simple look. What was even crazier, and was the entire problem, was the way she wanted to come completely undone with him. Despite every effort she'd made to tell herself it couldn't happen, to talk herself out of the ridiculous attraction she had for him, it wasn't working.

"Beth." She didn't have to look to know he was behind her

now. The heat coming off his body radiated into her. She stilled, and willed her breathing to calm. "Whatever this is between us, I know you feel it too."

She shook her head, more to convince herself than him.

Every fiber in her body strained to turn around and stop the pointless fighting within herself when it came to Slade. But she couldn't. A larger, stronger part of her was a mother of a twelve-year-old girl. She swallowed hard, forced her desire to simmer and turned. Instantly, she tried to take a step back, thrown off guard by his proximity. The scent of him filled her senses. The sheer intensity of him in her space.

"You do," he repeated.

She shook her head again, this time slower, in a halfhearted effort to ward him off. But at the same time her brain said no, her body said yes. Beth barely had to move forward and the second she did, he reached for her, closed the small gap between them and pulled her to him. His mouth crushed on to hers.

One hand slid up the side of her cheek and held her with a tenderness that belied the intensity of his kiss as his mouth explored hers.

Every argument she'd had against being with him was gone. She couldn't remember a thing as she gave in to him.

The moment didn't last long enough. When Slade stepped back, pulled his lips off hers with a gentle nip of her bottom lip, it was all she could do to restrain herself from taking another one.

Who was this woman? The transformation in her feelings was intense and confusing, and even a little exciting, especially because it'd happened so quickly.

"Now can you deny it?" He let his fingers trail down the side of her face, until he held her hand.

"You know I can't." She shook her head in an effort to what, deny it to herself?

"So go out with me. Before Friday. Before the skating. Just the two of us."

She wanted to. It didn't even surprise her with her intensity of longing, how much she did want to go out with him, and be a regular woman on a date with a man. Just for one night. But Slade was anything but regular and she had a child. And that was the reality of the situation. Despite how her body and emotions warred with her.

Beth took a step back and pulled her hand away from Slade. She needed distance, however minor, to think. She couldn't think straight with him touching her, his heat boring into her skin. "Even if I wanted to," she started, doing her best to control her voice so it wouldn't give her away, "I can't this week." It was a legitimate excuse. She had commitments every evening, even if she wasn't working and trying to raise a daughter. "I really can't. I would if I could." She surprised herself with the truth.

Slade reached out and brushed a droplet of water off her shoulder in an intimate, lingering touch. "I believe that's true." She thought he was going to kiss her again. Hell, she wanted him to kiss her again. Instead, he touched his finger to her lips. "I guess Friday will have to do."

Chapter Five

THE WEEK DRAGGED on for Slade. Every day that went by while he waited for Friday, and the chance to see Beth again, to arrive made him a little bit crazier. Every time he closed his eyes—heck, he didn't even have to close his eyes—he pictured the way her soft lips felt under his, and the way she finally gave in to the growing desire between them and kissed him back. And what a kiss it was.

Slade had kissed many women in his life, but never had one made him feel the way the smallest kiss from Beth made him feel. The week had been long and torturous at times, for sure, but it had also been productive. He'd spent the majority of the last four days writing. It had been years since he'd been so inspired and on such a songwriting roll. Max would be impressed.

If he'd told Max. Which he hadn't.

So far, his manager had called at least twice a day for an update. Slade knew Max was just looking out for him, and himself of course, but he wasn't ready to share his new music. Not yet. It was so different from anything else he'd put out in the past, he knew it was going to be met with resistance from Axel and the other guys in the group. But it didn't matter. The songs were good. Better than good. They were the best songs he'd ever written.

It was Beth.

Slade almost laughed at himself. It wasn't the first time he'd thought that the beautiful blond might be his muse. But the idea was ludicrous. He didn't believe in muses. Never had. But there was no other way to explain how she made him feel, how he'd felt from the moment he'd met her months earlier. She'd totally gotten under his skin, especially because he knew she felt the same way, but she kept fighting their attraction. It didn't make sense.

A knock on his hotel room door startled him out of his thoughts. He reached over and put his guitar down before he scanned the room and the mess he lived in. It wasn't fit for anyone to see, especially if he was disgusted by it. He kicked a dirty t-shirt out of the way. It wasn't unusual for him to shut himself off from the world when he got himself into the flow of writing, but he had to admit, the mess was excessive, even for him.

Slade opened the door to see Trent and Dylan on the other side with wary expressions on their faces.

"Hey guys." He stepped back into the room and held the door open for them. "What's up?"

The brothers shared a look before Dylan shrugged and stepped inside, followed by Trent. "We were just checking on you," Trent said.

"You know, to make sure you were alive."

"Alive?" Slade gathered up some of the dishes scattered on the unmade bed and piled them onto the room service cart. "Why would you say that?"

"No one's seen you all week." Trent stepped forward,

moved to sit on the couch, but at the last moment obviously thought better of it. "Have you been up here the whole time?"

Slade nodded.

"Who the hell is in charge of cleaning this room?" Dylan pulled out his cell phone. "I'm going to make sure Carmen talks to them. This is totally unacceptable."

Slade laughed and then, seeing that Dylan was serious, quickly said, "No. It's no one's fault. I put a hold on room service."

"You did what?" Dylan didn't even bother trying to hide the shock. He gestured around the space. "But…why?"

"I don't like being interrupted when I'm in the zone." For Slade it was simple, and not that terribly big of a deal, but looking at Trent and Dylan, he obviously was the only one who thought it was okay.

Trent shook his head slowly. "It's not good, man."

"It's really not." Dylan pressed some buttons on his phone. "I'm calling Carmen. She'll send someone up right away to take care of this."

"But I have to—"

"You have to come with us." Trent stepped forward. "Samantha mentioned that you'd be coming to the skating party tonight."

Slade nodded, a smile coming to play on his lips. He'd definitely be at that party, with the most beautiful woman in town.

"Right." Trent drew out the word. "Well, do you have skates? What about an actual winter jacket?"

His friend's words penetrated Slade's daydream of Beth and the sweet taste of her lips on his. He couldn't wait to get her in his arms again and in only a few hours—

"Wait." Slade turned to look at Trent. "What?"

"That's what I thought."

Dylan laughed. "More like what Sam thought."

"Whatever." Trent brushed off his brother's comment. "Doesn't matter. Either way, you're coming with us."

Slade glanced instinctively to his guitar. He still had more songs to write. Melodies to work on, lyrics to tighten. Part of him yearned to retreat back into his writing cave and get it done. But a bigger, much stronger part of him wanted—no, needed—to be with the subject of his writing. And to do that, Trent was right: he was going to need to prepare properly.

"Okay. Let's go."

"Oh hell no." Dylan held out his hand. "You're not going anywhere like that."

Trent chuckled. "Dylan's right. Shower and find some clean clothes. We'll meet you downstairs."

"But don't take too long. Carmen will kill me if I'm late tonight, and you do not want to mess with a pregnant woman." He raised an eyebrow.

"Trust me."

BETH HAD A BUSY WEEK. Between her clients and Jules, she'd barely had a moment to herself or to think about Slade. But just because she didn't have the time didn't mean that she didn't find it. Because she did. Every spare second Beth had, and even when she should have been focusing on her work, or helping Jules with multiplication, her mind drifted to Slade. His touch, his kiss, the way he looked at her. Or more to the point, the way he made her feel. She had no business feeling the way he made her feel. She was the mother of a twelve-year-old girl, and he was a rock star with a reputation. It couldn't happen. It was ridiculous. The problem was, the longer she had to think about it, the fewer objections she could come up with. Despite her best efforts to talk herself out of what had to be a bad idea, Beth couldn't think of very many reasons she shouldn't give in to what she was feeling with Slade.

Except for Jules. That was the one reason she could think of that held her back from acting on her building desires. Jules.

Or was that just an excuse?

She could no longer tell, and that was the whole problem.

"Hey." Jules came down the hall, out of her room, a long knit sweater and a cap on her head. "Are you ready to go? If we don't get there early, my friends are going to think I ditched them and then I won't be able to find them on the lake and—"

"I'm ready." Beth grabbed her own scarf and gloves and tugged her parka on over her sweater. "Is that all you're wearing? You're going to freeze."

Jules rolled her eyes in the way Beth was becoming all too familiar with. If twelve had this much attitude, she was in so much trouble when Jules became a teenager. "Whatever," Jules said with a shrug.

Beth had learned over the last few years to pick her battles. It wasn't her problem if Jules got cold. Not unless it took her away from her time with Slade. The thought popped up in her head before she knew it and she quickly pushed it out. She would not, could not, put her feelings or lust, or whatever it was, for Slade, come before her daughter. Even if it was just a skating party.

"Your choice," she said to her daughter and tried not to notice the thin leggings she was wearing. Maybe she'd be skating so hard she wouldn't notice the cold? Either way, it wasn't a fight she was willing to have. That would only delay their arrival to the party, and her time with Slade. And for the moment, that seemed a whole lot more important than another argument with Jules. "Let's go. You have your skates?"

"Yeah."

Beth took a breath and grabbed her own skates. "And some money, just in case you—"

"Yeah, Mom. I'm ready." Jules put her hand on her hip and Beth fought the urge to snap at her. It wouldn't help. Whatever it was that was going on with her daughter, one thing she knew for sure was that pushing her wasn't going to get her to open up.

"Okay." Beth forced a smile. "Let's get out of here then."

It wasn't too cold, at least not for a January night in the mountains, so they left the car at home and walked the short distance to Main Street, where immediately the festive spirit was in the air. Cedar Springs liked a party, and no matter what the excuse, the residents were out in force. Especially in January, when everyone was coming down from the Christmas excitement. It was the perfect time for a party, and in all her years living in Cedar Springs, Beth had never been more excited to tie up her skates and spend the night on the ice.

Beth had managed to get Jules talking on their walk, but as soon as they hit Main Street, her little girl clammed up again and searched for her friends. She tried not to be upset at her daughter's growing distance from her, but it was getting harder and harder. Particularly because she couldn't figure out why her little girl pulled away and in some moments, even seemed angry with her.

"There's Tori."

Beth turned to see Jules pointing to her friend, who stood next to her parents. Beth waved at them as Jules turned to her. "Can I go hang with Tori? Please?"

She didn't bother to hesitate or try to bargain with her. "Of course. But come and find me at eight, okay?"

Jules' face split into a smile and she jumped up on her toes to kiss Beth on the cheek. "Thanks, Mom."

Beth didn't even have time to process the shift in Jules before she was gone again. She watched her jog in Tori's direction and shook her head with a laugh. She had to laugh at the crazy mood changes of a pre-teen girl, otherwise she'd go insane. And it just seemed so much easier to laugh. It was also a solid survival strategy.

"Hey."

Beth spun to see her old friend, Rhys Anderson. "Hey yourself." Her smile was genuine as he bent down to kiss her on the cheek, as was their custom. Once there was a time when Beth thought they'd end up together, but they were better off friends and besides that, from the moment Kari Fox came to town, Rhys had been ridiculously and desperately in love with her. They were a much better match. "Where's Kari?"

"She's getting us some hot chocolate." He nodded his head in the direction of one of the stands that had been set up along the street. "Are you heading down to the lake?"

"Of course. I thought I'd try for my annual tie skates on, fall over and repeat performance. How about you guys?"

Rhys nodded. "I wouldn't miss the chance to introduce Kari to her first Cedar Springs skating party. It's tradition. Besides, I got the night off duty, so I plan to take full advantage of it." As one of the town's only police officers, Rhys was usually kept pretty busy, and it was nice to see him relaxing a little. "I hear you've been keeping company with rock stars lately."

His comment threw her off, and Beth blushed, thankful for the cool air that had already pinked her cheeks. The last thing she needed to explain was her and Slade. Especially considering there was nothing to explain. "Who told you that? Kari?"

"She might have mentioned something about it."

Beth shrugged. "I've said hi once or twice. That's about it."

The look on Rhys' face told her he was certainly not buying her explanations. But he wouldn't push it. Beth knew him well enough to know that. The corner of his mouth hitched up into a grin. "Looks like someone's coming to say hi again."

Beth spun on her heel, not even bothering to hide her

excitement, and it wasn't until she heard Rhys chuckle behind her that she realized she'd just given herself away. But it didn't matter, because Slade walked down the street. Dressed in a thigh-length wool coat and knit cap and with a pair of skates slung over his shoulder, he looked a lot less like a rock god guitar player, and a whole lot more like the boy-next-door, small-town hero type. Either way, she couldn't take her eyes off him and just watching him walk down the sidewalk, his own eyes locked onto her, completely oblivious of the people around him who pointed and whispered like star-struck fans at a concert, made her heart race.

Slade didn't have eyes for anyone but her, and he was locked on her, the heat in his gaze apparent even from a distance. But that heat only intensified when he got closer. He stopped in front of her, bent and offered her a chaste kiss on the cheek. So much like the one Rhys had given her, yet so different in all the ways that mattered. Her skin burned with the heat of his lips and when he pulled away and stared directly into her eyes, there was nowhere else for her to look. Slade held her with his intensity and it wasn't until Rhys cleared his throat loudly and obviously that Beth blinked.

"Hi." Rhys thrust his hand out to Slade, who shook it with a smile. "I'm Rhys, a good friend of Beth's." There was a trace of something in Rhys' voice. A warning? Beth almost laughed at the idea. It was no secret that Rhys and Beth were close, and for him to be protective of her wouldn't be too far of a stretch, but it had been so long since Beth had any kind of date or anything that remotely resembled a date, that Rhys probably had no idea what he was supposed to protect her from.

"Good to meet you." Slade's smile was genuine, but Beth didn't miss the flicker of disapproval in Rhys' eyes when Slade moved so he stood next to her. She could feel the heat of him next to her, even through her parka. But maybe that was just her, and the increased heat he caused in her being so close?

After their introduction, the two men stared at each other awkwardly, in a sort of showdown, that didn't make any sense at all to Beth and would have been laughable had she not already been so nervous to see Slade again. For whatever reason, she hadn't seen him around the Springs all week, and even though she'd told herself it didn't mean anything and that he couldn't be avoiding her because of the kiss they'd shared, there was still a small insecure part of her that said he was.

"Well," she said after a moment. "We should probably get down to the lake. The fire should be going by now." Slade looked down at her and his hand reached out to twine his fingers through hers. "Are you ready?"

"Absolutely."

"You guys go ahead. Kari should be done in a second and we'll meet you down there."

Beth nodded and glanced over to where Jules and her group of friends had gathered. For a moment, she had the idea that she should go tell her daughter they were heading to the lake, but then thought better of it. She'd let her enjoy the evening with her friends. Jules wasn't a baby anymore and as hard as it was letting go, it was also a good thing. She squeezed Slade's hand. "Okay. We'll see you there."

Main Street was packed with what had to be every resident of Cedar Springs. They stood around, sipped hot chocolate, chatted and laughed. Everyone was in a party mood, which was the whole point of the evening, and it made Beth proud to be part of such a great town. She hadn't been sure whether moving back to Cedar Springs was the best move for them and despite Jules experiencing a few bumps in the road, for the most part it had been good. With Slade at her side, holding her hand, they attracted more than a few stares from people as they made their way down to the ice.

"I'm sorry about Rhys," she said when they'd moved far

enough away. "He's really a good guy. Don't let him be too hard on you."

"Hard on me?" Slade chuckled. "That's nothing. Besides, he's just being a good friend. He obviously cares about you quite a bit."

She nodded. "He does."

Slade squeezed her hand. He stopped and turned her gently into him. "I care about you, too." He spoke quietly, his voice low and full of meaning that Beth couldn't even begin to decipher. With his free hand, he tipped her chin up and leaned down to plant a soft, gentle kiss on her lips.

The kiss couldn't have been any sweeter, but passion burned through her veins and sparked something deep inside her. But it was his words that affected her. He cared about her? He barely knew her.

She pulled back and laughed. "People are watching. Let's go skate." She turned and tugged his hand to lead him to a bench where they could tie up their skates.

Whatever it was that she felt for him, it couldn't be anything more serious than a little fun. And whatever it was that he was playing at, Beth was determined to keep it light. It was so much safer that way.

ICE-SKATING on a frozen lake was so far from the type of thing Slade usually did for fun that he wasn't quite sure how he should behave. And after Trent and Dylan had taken him to the only sporting goods shop in town and outfitted him with what they insisted was proper attire for the mountains, he'd started to feel nervous about seeing Beth and trying to fit in. It was ridiculous, mostly because he was never nervous. He could get up in front of tens of thousands of people and perform without a flicker of nerves, but throw him into a small-town skating party, and he was like a teenage boy all over again.

As crazy as it sounded, it was probably better that they were in a crowd of people, because at least he was used to that. As for Beth, the way she made him feel, was inexplicable, and if he didn't get to kiss those sweet lips again, and soon, he would not be held responsible for his actions.

"I never asked." Her voice broke through his thoughts and he looked over to see her tightening the laces on her skate. "Do you know how to skate?" Her mischievous smile told him that she certainly didn't expect him to be able to hold his own on the ice.

"I know the basics."

"The basics?"

He shrugged and pulled on his brand new skates. They were stiff and in serious need of being broken in, but he didn't have much of a choice. "I'm sure I'll be okay."

She laughed. "Because you can do anything, right?"

He finished tying his laces and gave her a wink. "Of course. Don't you know that celebrities are good at everything? It's part of the code."

"The code?"

Slade quickly put his second skate on while he spoke. "Of course, it's the celebrity code. We're pretty much supposed to be amazing at everything. You know, just in case anyone's watching."

Her laugh filled his senses. Making her smile was quickly becoming one of his favorite things. "Well, Mr. Celebrity." She got to her feet and made her way through the snow to the ice, where she pushed off into a smooth turn. "Let's see what you've got."

He took his time. Slade carefully tucked his boots under the bench and pushed up. He wobbled a little on his blades, and picked his way carefully over to the ice, where he took a couple hesitant skate-steps and crashed into her. Beth staggered back-wards but was able to steady herself quickly, even with his arms wrapped around her.

"What were you saying about being good at everything?"

He shrugged, and pulled her closer. "Maybe I just wanted to hold you?" He stole a kiss before she could laugh again. Her lips were cool from the night air, but they instantly melded to his as they both sank into the kiss that was much deeper than the one earlier. Before he could lose himself completely in her, Slade pulled away. "Because that was pretty good, too."

Beth shook her head with a smile.

"You disagree?"

"I didn't say that." She untangled herself from him. "But we came here to skate. So come on. I'll show you a few things and you'll be a pro in no time, Mr. Celebrity."

He let Beth take him by the hand and lead him farther out onto the ice, which had been cleared of snow to create a wide skating rink. There was another cleared rink with nets on either end where a hockey game was going on. Large poles with lights had been set up around the rink so the players could see the puck, and benches full of spectators who cheered on their friends lined the edge.

"Okay." Beth released his hand. "It's really pretty easy once you get the hang of it. But if you push with one foot and let yourself glide a little, you'll start to build a smooth rhythm. Then put your other foot down and do the same." She skated around him in an easy circle and he spun slowly, following her progress. "Easy. Right?"

He shrugged.

"Ready to try?" Beth came to a stop in front of him, and he had to resist the urge to kiss her again. Even bundled up in a winter coat, she was stunning.

Slade nodded and clapped his gloved hands together. "Why not?"

She skated backwards, kept her eyes on him and held out her arms the way she might to a small child learning to take his first steps. "Okay, you can do it. Just one step and glide."

He did as she suggested, moving towards her on a shaky leg, and was rewarded by a smile. So he did it again.

Beth clapped her hands together and smiled. "You're doing awesome."

"I think I'm ready for something harder."

Her smile twisted into a frown. "Harder?"

Slade swallowed his own smile and tried to appear as focused and serious as possible. "Yeah. Like…maybe…" With a strong push-off, he accelerated and as soon as he had a little speed, turned easily into a quick spin before accelerating again and skating an easy figure eight around Beth. When he was finished, he came to a quick stop hockey style, showering ice shavings over her legs and looked down at her shocked face.

"You…" She shook her head. "What…"

"I'm a pretty quick learner, huh?" He laughed. "I told you it was part of the celebrity code. We're good at everything."

Realization crossed Beth's face as her brain obviously caught up with the trick he'd played on her. "You're such a jerk." She pushed a gloved hand at his shoulder and shoved him back slightly on his skates, but Slade only laughed harder and grasped her hand in his.

"You should have seen your face," he teased. The surprise in her eyes had been worth his little joke. And it had been too long since he'd laughed so hard. Beth brought out a playful side in him that he'd forgotten about for too long while he was busy trying to be a famous musician. And he liked it.

"Oh yeah?" Beth narrowed her eyes, but her lips played up in a grin that told Slade he was going to pay for his little joke. "Well, wait until you see my face when I beat you to the other side of the rink."

Before he could even agree to the race, she took off. For a

woman who was shorter than him by at least a foot, she was strong. And fast. It took Slade a few moments to catch up with her and for a split second the thought crossed his mind that he should let her win their little friendly race. But his competitive edge took over and he passed her. A quick glance behind him told Slade he'd made the right choice. Determination lined Beth's face as she pumped her arms faster, trying to catch him. There was no doubt that she liked a challenge and he was definitely the man to give it to her.

He faced forward again, just in time to swerve around a group of young girls who giggled and squealed as he passed. He could hear Beth right behind him. It wasn't going to be an easy race to win, that was for sure. He was out of practice and she was determined. The snowbank that marked the end of the shoveled ice rink and the finish line was only a few feet away. Slade dug deep, pushed his left leg back while he drove himself forward. But instead of propelling him faster across the ice and towards the finish line, the tip of his blade caught a crack in the frozen lake and he stumbled forward as if in slow motion.

Right before he made impact with the snowbank—that he was hoping was as soft as it looked—he felt a thud on his back as Beth ran into him, and together they fell into the snow. Instinctively, he reached out and wrapped his arms around her as they rolled through the snow. When they came to a stop, Slade found himself on his back and looking up into Beth's snow-covered face.

The moment she opened her eyes and saw him, likely equally snow covered, they both burst out laughing. He held her close while her body shook against his, but soon his own laughter melted away, replaced firmly by desire. The effect of having her body pressed up so close against his was strong, undeniable, and definitely no laughing matter. She noticed him staring at her, and swallowed her laughter.

"I guess we both won."

"Oh," he said, his voice rough and thick with desire, "I'd say I definitely won." He reached up and with a snow-covered hand, pulled her mouth down to his. Their kiss could have melted the snow they were laying in, things between them were so hot. It didn't seem to matter whether they stood half-naked in a steamy hot pool, or covered in thick layers in a pile of snow. The passion between them was only getting stronger, and Slade was having a hard time controlling himself.

"Hey! Are you guys okay?"

Beth broke the kiss at the sound of voices and people skating towards them, but she didn't move away. And Slade could see the heat reflected in her eyes as she gave him one last lingering look before she called out.

"We're fine."

SAM DROPPED to her knees in the snowbank next to where Beth lay, still cradled in Slade's arms. "Are you okay? That was a crazy wipeout. What the hell were you guys doing?"

"Racing," Slade said simply, still looking at Beth.

Sam looked between the two of them and shook her head. "You're both crazy."

"Come on." Beth heard Trent's voice, as she felt herself get lifted off Slade and set easily on her feet. She instantly missed the heat of his body, and his desire that she could feel, even through the layers of winter clothes between them.

"Thanks," she muttered in Trent's direction before she brushed the snow off her body. He'd already turned to offer a hand to Slade, who took it and came to a stand next to him.

"You're sure you guys are okay?" Sam directed the question to both of them, but stared directly at Beth while she asked. No doubt there was a lot more behind the question and

Beth knew her best friend well enough to know exactly what she was asking.

She reached over and took Slade's hand in hers. She gave him a tug and pulled him towards her. All of Beth's friends undoubtedly had a million questions they were dying to ask her. Beth grinned devilishly, and knowing that Sam would get her alone later and grill her, she asked as casually as she could, "Who wants hot chocolate?"

Together, the four of them skated over to the bonfire that blazed in the middle of the ice. When she was a kid, Beth had always been worried it would melt the ice and they'd all sink into the water despite the dozen times or more that it was explained to her it was perfectly safe, and the ice was too thick for the fire—which looked impressive, but actually burned at a lower temperature than she would expect—to melt through two feet of ice.

Sam had her head waitress, Kylie, selling hot chocolate at the Grizzly Paw booth with the proceeds going to local charities and next to that was Suzy Crosswell and the Dream Puffs table loaded with a variety of cookies.

"How about we get the hot chocolate?" Trent gestured to Slade. "You girls can find us a spot next to the fire."

Before Beth could protest, Slade's hand slipped out of hers and Sam dragged her towards the fire. They managed to find an open space with a few hay bales that were close enough to keep warm, but not so close that they were in the middle of everything. The moment they sat down, Sam whirled around and fired questions at her. "What's going on with you and Slade? How long has it been going on? Is it a secret? Have you slept with him? What does Jules think?"

Beth laughed and used the distraction to attempt to formulate her thoughts. "I don't know, a few days, probably not, hell no, and I don't know that either."

"What?"

"The answer to your questions." Beth tried to be casual, but with Sam practically bouncing out of her seat, it was getting to be increasingly difficult to keep her composure.

Sam's hands fluttered in front of her face. "Wait. Slow down. I thought you said there was nothing going on between you two. That—what was it you said exactly?" She tapped her finger against her temple as she pretended to think. "Oh yeah." She pointed her finger at Beth. "You said there was no way you would ever or could ever have a relationship with a rock star."

"It's not a relationship." Beth picked at a piece of hay sticking out of the bale. She was happy for the dim lighting because she knew her best friend would see the confusion all over her face. It wasn't a relationship. Of course it wasn't. But that hadn't stopped Beth's imagination from skipping all over the place, wondering "what if."

"And you haven't slept with him?"

Beth's head shot up. "God no. I can't just—"

"Why not? He's gorgeous. And if the tabloids are to be believed—"

"They're not."

Sam winked. "But if they were…"

Beth shook her head and laughed. "I can't sleep with him. I'm not…" She drifted off. She wasn't what? She was a young woman who had desires and dammed if she didn't have them for Slade in a really bad way. But she was also a mother and it wasn't as if she could just bring some guy home with her daughter. She shook her head, trying more to convince herself than her friend.

As it turned out, Sam didn't need any convincing. "I don't know if you remember," she said. "But it wasn't that long ago that Archer was busy trying to convince me to lighten up a little and have some fun. Sleeping together doesn't mean getting married. It just means—"

"I know what it means." And she did. Oh, did she ever. It

meant quenching that fire within her that had been burning since the very moment Slade Black and his sexy voice had rolled into town. And dammed if she didn't want to quench that fire. Consequences be dammed.

"So what are you waiting for? It's pretty obvious he's into you."

She felt like a teenager needing validation when she asked, "You think so?" It was a stupid question and they both knew it. Beth wasn't blind. She could see just as easy as everyone else in town that Slade was into her. More than into her. He wanted her with an urgency that both scared and fueled her all at the same time.

Sam didn't even bother to answer the question. She raised her eyebrows and gave Beth a knowing look. "So what's the hangup? You obviously like him, too."

Beth glanced quickly over her shoulder and saw Slade surrounded by fans while Trent stood by and held the hot chocolate. And wasn't that the problem right there? He was a celebrity. It's not as if she could have any kind of life with him. Reading her mind, Sam said, "That shouldn't matter."

Beth turned to face her friend. "But it does." She took a breath and blinked hard at the sudden and totally unexpected tears that pricked at her eyelids. She never cried, especially over a man. She swiped at her face. "I don't just want a one-night stand, Sam. I want it all." She didn't add that she wanted what Sam and Trent, Rhys and Kari, and Dylan and Carmen had; that went without saying. "It's time."

Sam laughed and squeezed her arm. "Hell, it's long past time," she said. "And you'll have it, Beth." Her laughter died, and her voice grew serious. "But don't close off the opportunity just because of what someone does for a living."

Beth shook her head. "No. It's—"

"It is." Sam waved her hand. "Besides, why are we even

having this conversation? It obviously isn't very serious if you guys haven't even had sex. Talk to me when it gets real."

Real. Beth laughed for Sam's benefit, but inside all she could think was just how real things with Slade felt. It may still be new, but he stirred feelings in her she'd never had before. And if that wasn't real, she didn't know what was.

"Until then, don't say anything to Jules. I don't want her—"

"Don't want me to what?"

Both women spun around to see Jules, her arms crossed as she stood behind them. How long had she been there? Beth was grateful for the shadows, so her daughter couldn't read her face and the guilt that must be written all over it. When people told her how hard it would be to be a single mother, they hadn't focused much beyond the baby years. Dating with a pre-teen: that's when things got hard.

"Hey." Sam rescued the situation. "Are you having fun?" Jules nodded, but still didn't take her eyes off her mother. "Any cute guys?" That made Jules laugh and drop down on the hay bale next to Sam.

"You wouldn't believe it, Auntie Sam, but there are like no cute boys in this town."

Beth smiled to herself. Jules had always responded better to Sam than her. But that's probably because Sam got to be the fun "Auntie" while she had to be the heavy. Having Jules as a teenager hadn't been easy, but she had definitely gotten by with the love and support of her friends. And even when she felt a little envious of Sam and Jules' connection, she was still thankful for it. Particularly if it took the heat off her.

Sam laughed. "You know what? I would believe it. It was the same way when I was your age. No decent boys at all."

"Who isn't decent?" Trent skated over with two hot choco-lates. He handed one to Sam and pulled up another bale of hay to sit on. "Your boyfriend over there is exhausting." Beth glared at him and Sam smacked him and spilled his drink over his jacket, but it was too late.

"Your boyfriend?" Jules turned to face Beth, her face hard with question in only the way a twelve-year-old girl could pull off. "Slade Black is your boyfriend?"

"No."

"Then why—"

"Because he's an idiot," Sam jumped in. Trent shrugged and tried without much success to wipe the chocolate from his jacket.

"Slade and I are just friends," Beth said. "We like spending time together. That's all."

Jules narrowed her eyes and stared at her mom for a second before she shook her head. "Good. Because it would be so uncool if you were dating him."

"How would that be uncool?" Sam asked. "I can't think of anything much cooler than your mom dating a rock star."

Jules groaned and got to her feet. "If you don't know why, I'm not even going to tell you. I just came over here to ask you if I can sleep at Tori's tonight. A bunch of us are going to go over there and watch a movie. If it's okay with you," she added quickly.

As full of attitude as Jules was lately, at least towards her, she was still a good kid. "Of course. Be home by noon, okay?"

"Thanks, Mom." Jules bent down and kissed Beth quickly on the cheek before she skated away.

Beth watched in shock as she skated by Slade, who reached out and gave her a high five as she passed. Jules called something to him that Beth couldn't make out and joined her friends.

"Talk about mood swings," Sam said. "Were we ever like that?"

Beth laughed, mostly because if she didn't laugh, she might

cry from the frustration of it all. "There's no way we were ever that bad. I keep thinking this stage will pass."

"It will, and then she'll be a teenager." They laughed together and it wasn't until Slade finally joined them after satisfying his adoring fans that Beth realized with Jules out of the house, there was no reason she couldn't do as Sam suggested and make things a bit more real with Slade.

Chapter Six

SLADE DIDN'T REALIZE how nice it could be to sit next to a bonfire, his arm around a beautiful girl, hold her close, and drink a simple hot chocolate. It had been so long since he'd participated in any activity so pure and wholesome that he didn't think he was actually capable of it. And besides a few moments when he needed to sign autographs, the whole evening was so normal and easy, that he even allowed himself a few seconds of daydreaming. What would it be like to actually live in Cedar Springs?

He knew he was getting ahead of himself, especially where Beth was concerned. But he was used to getting exactly what he wanted, when he wanted it. And what he wanted, at least at that moment, was the woman who leaned up next to him, her gentle weight pressing into him, heating him in ways he was going to need to deal with.

As if she knew he was thinking about her, she tipped her head up so he could see her sweet, sexy smile. "You're awfully quiet," she said.

"I'm just enjoying the fire." He ran a gloved finger down the side of her cheek and lowered his mouth to hers. Damn, he'd wanted her. It wasn't safe to kiss her like that, at least not in public. Reluctantly, he pulled back. "I can't do that," he said. "Not here."

Her grin was devilish. "Well, let's go somewhere else."

Slade didn't need to be asked twice. Without unwrapping his arm from around her, he stood and pulled Beth with him.

"We're going to go for another skate," Beth told her friends. They both raised a hand and sent them off. Slade was pretty sure he'd seen Sam give Trent a knowing look, but he didn't care.

The last thing Slade wanted to do was skate some more, but when Beth took his hand and started skating to the far end of the shoveled rink, he kept pace with her. "You really did want to skate some more," he said after they'd made a few laps.

"No." She shook her head. "Skating is actually the last thing I want to do."

"Then, why—"

She came to a stop so suddenly, Slade had to let go of her hand, and circle back so he didn't pull her over. When he came to a stop in front of her, he couldn't read the expression on her face. "What? Are you—"

Her lips were on his in a hungry kiss he wasn't prepared for but took as greedily as he could. He pulled her close to him, pressed her body up against the front of him. There were too many layers of clothing between them. Slade slid one hand down to rest on her ass, squeezing her even closer, while his other hand held the base of her neck. He wasn't going to let her go; he couldn't. He needed her with an urgency that threatened to consume him.

They were at the edge of the shoveled ice, where the lights were definitely dimmer, the shadows longer, and while he didn't care that they were in full view of anyone who cared to look over and see them, he recognized that Beth might. Especially after her daughter had high-fived him earlier and reminded him, "Don't forget she's my mom." And he wouldn't forget, at least not until he had her alone.

With excruciating effort, he pulled away from her and looked at her desire-drenched face. Her breaths came in short puffs; her chest rose and fell with the passion that was palpable between them.

"We shouldn't do this here." He took her hands and held them in his much larger, gloved hands. He needed to feel her, but it was the only contact between them he dared risk.

She shook her head. "No. You're right."

He prepared himself for her to say goodnight and leave, the way she had the last time. Never had he wanted a woman so bad and had her continue to deny the connection between them. Hell, never had he wanted a woman so bad, period. "I want you so bad," he growled. "I'm not going to let you leave. Not again."

Her eyes held his with as much intensity as he felt. "Do you always get what you want?" There was a slight tease in her tone, but her face gave away nothing.

"Yes."

Her eyes flared with the challenge but she didn't look away. "What about what I want?"

With great effort, Slade controlled his breath. "I'm willing to bet we want the same thing."

"Jules is sleeping at a friend's house." She practically whispered the words, but they were all he needed to hear. Slade turned and without releasing her hands, skated slowly towards the bench where they'd left their shoes.

BETH DIDN'T LIVE FAR off Main Street, but never before had that short distance felt like a hundred miles. They barely spoke as they made their way through the crowd, hand in hand, stopping only to say a quick hello to friends and neighbors. As soon as they turned off Main Street onto Beth's street, she allowed herself a second to think about what she was doing. Dozens of people had seen her with Slade at the party. Jules already suspected something was going on between them. Surely by morning, the entire town would know that they left together and…so what?

The sudden indifference shocked her. She'd always been a woman who played by the rules. At least ever since Jules had been born. She'd seen firsthand what breaking the rules would get her and as much as she loved her daughter, there were definitely things she'd do over again if she could. But in that moment, with Slade holding her hand so tightly that she could feel his heat through their gloves, Beth didn't care.

She led him up the walk to her front door and stuck the key in the lock. Before she could turn it, Slade grabbed her and in one strong motion, flipped her around and pressed her into the door.

"You're sure she's out for the night?" he whispered roughly in her ear. Desire flooded her. If he hadn't held her up with his body pressed so tightly to hers, her legs might have given out completely.

"Yes." She managed to get the word out and it was all Slade needed. He reached around her, twisted the key in the lock, pushed the door open, and moved her backwards into the house.

She heard the door close behind her somehow as he pushed her up against the wall. He pinned her with his mouth; their tongues crashed together in a need that had been building for too long. She'd thought their kisses were loaded with passion before, but even they were tame compared to what happened between them now. Her body trembled with need as Slade managed to get his hands between them long enough to unzip her jacket and pull it down over her shoulders. Somehow she pulled her lips away from his long enough to pull her sweater over her head before she claimed his mouth once again.

It was when he unzipped her jeans, and guided them over her hips, that she froze. She pulled her head back, gasped for breath and squeezed her eyes shut.

"Beth. I'll stop if you want me to." Slade's voice was strained. She knew he would stop if she asked him to. It would require great restraint, but she knew he would. "What do you want?"

She opened her eyes, and tried to focus on him. His eyes were dark with desire and want. Every part of her body told her what to do, what she wanted. Her chest heaved with every breath as she tried to slow her mind long enough to figure out her thoughts. His touch on her felt so right, and how could something that felt so right be wrong? And even if it was, Beth realized she didn't give a damn.

"I want this," she whispered. And then louder, "I want you."

In response, Slade bent down, tugged her boots off her feet, and slid her jeans down her legs. When she was naked, less her panties and bra, he stood slowly. He ran his hands up along her body until he stood and stared at her with hunger in his eyes. "You're so beautiful." She blushed, and Slade must have sensed her hesitancy because he added, "You're absolutely perfect." Her entire body trembled, more from his words and the look in his eyes as he spoke them than the cool air that pricked her skin.

They still stood in the hallway, only she was the only one undressed. Slade had stripped out of his boots and jacket, but was still frustratingly fully dressed in his signature black t-shirt and his jeans slung low on his hips. She reached out, ready to remedy the problem but he stopped her as he clasped her wrist in his strong hand.

"No," he said. "Not yet." He took her other wrist and raised both her hands over her head, pressed her against the wall with his body before he used his mouth to trail kisses down her neck. She'd never before felt so controlled and at the mercy of someone else, and her blood ran hot in her veins as she strained against his tight grip. She arched her neck to give him better access. He lifted his face to meet her eyes. "I'm going to release your hands." She nodded, although he hadn't actually asked a question. "But you have to promise to keep them to yourself."

At that moment, she would have done anything he asked as long as he kept touching her and kissing her. Anything to relieve the ache that built up in her core and between her legs.

When he released her, Beth's arms fell to her sides, and she splayed her fingers against the wall, looking for purchase as Slade took his kisses farther down her body. He stopped at the swell of her breasts. He used his thumbs to graze roughly over her hard nipples, pressed against the lace of her bra. A groan escaped her lips as he sucked first one into his mouth, through the fabric of her bra, and then the other.

He didn't release her from her bra, but left her panting against the wall as he continued to travel down her body. His hands slid over the curve of her hips to the elastic of her matching lace panties.

Beth barely stopped herself from begging him to slide the scrap of fabric down. She'd never felt so wanton and desperate for a man to touch her the way she craved Slade's touch on her. But she couldn't pretend to fight the desire that burned in her, especially when there was no doubt he felt the same way. Definitely not, she thought again as he pressed his lips to the hollow of her stomach, directly above where she burned for him to touch her. Beth bit her lip to keep from crying out her demand.

His fingers traced the lace elastic of her panties, and painfully, slowly edged closer to her heat. She pressed further into the wall in an effort to still her body from the tremors that built deep in her core. How was it that he hadn't even touched her yet and she thought she might come completely undone? Had it really been so long since she'd been with a man this way?

She bit down on her bottom lip as Slade's hands slid around her back side and pulled her into him. When he kissed her through her already soaked panties, Beth couldn't fight back the cry that escaped her mouth. She threw her head back and arched her back into the orgasm that took her completely by surprise. If Slade hadn't had a firm grip on her buttocks, surely her legs would have given out as she rode out the climax.

Never in her life, and her somewhat minimal experience, had she ever experienced a climax so completely unexpected, quick, and totally shattering. Beth was pretty sure her legs wouldn't be able to hold her up. When she lifted her head and opened her eyes, she was surprised to see Slade standing in front of her now, his hands firmly on her waist, a satisfied grin on his handsome face.

"I'm...I..." She shook her head. There were no words. At least none she could find.

He laughed and kissed her gently on the lips. But what started as a small kiss quickly morphed into something with much more urgency behind it. When Slade wrapped his arms around her and drew her close again, her bare skin scraped roughly against his jeans. Beth was shocked to realize he was still fully dressed. And by the hot heat pressing into her belly, he was clearly not finished with her. Which was more than okay with her, she realized as she twisted her fingers through his hair and deepened the kiss further.

SHE WAS GOING to be the death of him. From the moment Slade undressed Beth and exposed her perfectly soft, curvy body, he knew he was in trouble. No way would one night with her be enough. Not nearly enough. He hadn't planned to push her up against the wall and make her scream right there in the entryway of her house, but dammed if he could stop himself once he got started.

Beth was so responsive to his every touch it was if she was in tune with him, and his own needs. He couldn't even begin to explain what she did to him. Especially because there was no way he could explain it himself. What he did know was if he didn't get her out of the hallway and into a bed soon, he would take her right there on the rug and she deserved better than that.

With great effort, he pulled away from her sweet mouth. Her lips were swollen, slightly parted and begging for more. Slade swallowed back a groan. "Bedroom," was all he managed to get out before he claimed her mouth again. She was like a drug, and if he didn't get his fix soon, he knew he would lose control completely.

Not giving her the opportunity to answer, he lifted her under her buttocks so she could wrap her legs around him. He broke the kiss long enough to look up and navigate his way down the hall, through to a small living room and beyond into what looked like a hallway that led to bedrooms. While he carried her, she kept her mouth busy as she nibbled on his neck, and pressed her body against his, rubbed herself teasingly against him.

She had no idea what fire she played with and the second he found a suitable bed to deposit her on, there was no doubt he would show her exactly what she did to him.

He was about to open the first doorway he came to, when Beth raised her head from his neck long enough to mumble, "Next one." It only took him the span of a few seconds before he found the next door and pushed into her bedroom. The scent of her surrounded him, fueled his passion, as he crossed the room to the bed where he deposited her onto her back.

Beth looked up at him, a sexy glint in her eyes and a wicked little smile on her face. She was unbelievably hot in her chaste white lace panties and bra set. But she didn't fool him. He knew she wasn't an innocent angel, not judging from the way she kissed him, and the way she'd shattered against him moments earlier.

She leaned back on her elbows, pushed her breasts out so they strained against the lace of her bra. "You're wearing far too many clothes."

"I was just thinking the same thing about you." Like a cat on the prowl, he began a slow predatory crawl up the bed, his eyes firmly locked on his target.

But before he could reach her, Beth put a foot up and pressed it against his shoulder. "Not so fast." She licked her lip, slowly, drawing out the move. "I want to see you."

There was no way he was going to argue with her. Not when she looked the way she did, her chest heaving from the passion he'd stirred in her. Slade sat back on his heels and crooked his finger to beckon her. Beth obliged and in a moment, knelt in front of him. Without waiting for an invitation, she slid her hands under the tight fabric of his shirt, trailed her hands up over his chest and pulled the cotton with her.

A chill ran through him as she painstakingly slid the t-shirt all the way up and over his head. The look in her beautiful blue eyes was pure hunger, and she took her time as she looked at him. "Nice," she said.

Slade knew he looked good. His manager had insisted on the many hours that he put in at the gym every week, ensured his fans always liked what they saw. But to have Beth approve meant more than what any random fan thought. A whole lot more. "That's it?" he teased.

"There's still a whole lot more to see." She bit her bottom lip again and there was an answering tug low in Slade's belly. Damn, she didn't even know how hot she was. Especially when she let herself go.

Not willing to make her wait, Slade jumped to his feet, still standing on the bed, and quickly unbuttoned his jeans. He pulled them down with his underwear until he stood naked in front of her. Over her. He looked down at her, the lust he felt for her matched on her face. He needed her. Needed to see those eyes look up at him while he was inside her.

"And now?"

In response, Beth pulled him down to her, on top of her. She wrapped her legs around him and ground her hips against him. "Perfect," she whispered in his ear.

Her voice was almost his complete undoing. He lifted himself up just enough to pull her panties off and unclasp her bra so her beautiful breasts were displayed for him. His mouth was on her again, his hands everywhere. He craved the contact between them. "Beth, I—"

She cut him off with another kiss, this one more intense than any other. There could be no more words between them. The time for talking was long over. He pulled away from her long enough to dig a condom out of the back pocket of his discarded jeans and slide it on.

He held himself on his elbows so he didn't crush her, and then he entered her quickly with one powerful thrust. He filled her completely. Her eyes squeezed shut, and Slade froze. He traced her jaw with a finger and stroked his thumb as gently as he could over her lips. "Open your eyes." His voice was strained, but he needed to see her. "Look at me, Beth."

Just when he thought they wouldn't, Beth's eyelids fluttered open, her normally clear blue eyes dark with the passion between them. She fixed her gaze on him, and it was almost the ruin of him.

"I want to see you." He moved his hips in a gentle rhythm. "I need to."

A small mewling sound came out of her, and she wrapped her legs around his back to drive him in closer.

He couldn't fight the intensity between them, and eyes locked, together they rode to a shattering climax. Slade felt her release seconds before his own. Neither of them looked away, sharing each other's passion with the other.

Their chests rose and fell in unison, but Slade couldn't force himself to release his grip on her. He bent and placed a chaste kiss on her forehead. "You," he said softly, "are totally unlike any woman I've ever met."

In response, she squeezed her eyes and turned her head to the side. Maybe she thought it was just a line, but for the life of him, Slade had never met anyone quite like her before. No woman had ever gotten so completely under his skin the way Beth had. And that both thrilled him and scared the hell out of him.

Chapter Seven

THERE WERE SO many things she could be thinking, should be thinking, with Slade lying next to her when Beth woke the next morning. His arm was wrapped around her and held her into his chest, where her head rested. Despite the solid muscle beneath her, she was surprisingly comfortable, and more than a little content. Sure, there were all types of things she should be thinking about the night they'd spent together, but the only thing she could focus on was how happy she felt.

The sun peeked through the curtains, which meant it was probably almost seven in the morning. Late for her to be getting up and getting started with her day, but for the life of her, she couldn't make herself move. A total body exhaustion consumed her, despite the few hours of sleep they'd managed to get between lovemaking sessions.

Beth instantly chastised herself. She couldn't call sex with a rock star lovemaking. She couldn't even afford to think of it that way. As wild and wonderful and totally unlike anything she'd ever experienced before, it wasn't love. It was sex. And she'd do well to remember that. She may have convinced herself for the night that she was okay with a one-night stand, a casual fling, and hell, she was glad she had. It was a night she'd remember forever, but that's all it was.

Before she could stop it, a tear slid from her eye, and landed on Slade's skin. She cursed herself under her breath. It must be all the heightened emotions from so many climaxes. Her body wasn't used to such activity. That was why she reacted the way she was. Not because of anything else. To think it was anything more was ridiculous, and she wasn't some silly girl who made situations into something they weren't. She'd never been that girl. But despite all the pragmatism in the world, she couldn't help but be sad that she would probably never feel the way Slade had made her feel, again.

"Good morning, beautiful."

She spun her head around and looked directly in his dark eyes. "How is it that you look so rested?" She grinned. "I'm exhausted."

His hand trailed along her naked back, down her spine where it came to rest on her bottom. "Well, that's a shame." His fingers made slow, sensual circles on her ass cheek. "I was thinking of—"

"Oh, I don't think so." She shut him down before she had the chance to give in to what she wanted so badly as well. One night, that's all she could allow herself. It's all she could logi-cally allow herself if she wanted to protect Jules and herself from unnecessary hurt and speculation. It was bad enough she'd gone home with him last night in front of pretty much the entire town.

He turned, so she lay on her back while he loomed over her. His sexy eyes flirted with her. "I can't convince you…" His kiss was both soft and heavy with heat, and Beth's resolve was tested. She answered his kiss, and wrapped a hand around his neck.

Slade was so good at convincing her that she would have changed her mind completely if there hadn't been a loud growl coming from the direction of her belly in that instant. He pulled back and gave her a sideways glance. "Was that your—"

She laughed. "I guess I'm a little hungry."

Grateful for the distraction, Beth rolled out from under him and snatched her robe from the floor. It was clear that she was no match for him, and the effect he had on her. There was no point making what would only be a difficult situation even messier.

Before she could slip out the door and out to the kitchen, he reached out and a strong hand grasped her wrist and pulled her to stop.

"Hey."

She looked down into his eyes, a moment ago sparkling with laughter, now dark and serious. "I meant what I said last night." He yanked her down with just enough force and placed a kiss on her lips. "Let me make you breakfast. I never get a chance to cook."

He looked so genuine, she couldn't help but return his smile. "Okay." She nodded. It had been a very long time since someone cooked for her, and she didn't count the blackened toast Jules made for her every Mother's Day. "That would be nice."

"Good." He kissed her again, and Beth allowed herself a moment to think about how nice it would be to wake up like that every morning. She pushed it away before the idea could take root. "Go have a shower, and when you're finished, I'll have breakfast ready."

The offer was too good to turn down, so Beth left Slade to his own devices in her kitchen and headed into the bathroom.

She took her time under the hot spray; she lathered her body and stretched every muscle, sore from use. It had been a long time since she'd felt a man's touch on her skin, even longer since she'd experienced the sweet ache of a long night. And never before had Beth felt quite so, so... satisfied. She turned under the spray, and relived Slade's insistent fingers as he worked the pleasure from her.

She didn't want to overanalyze the situation or make something out of nothing, particularly when there was nothing to be had from the situation. And that was what she focused on as she rinsed the shampoo from her hair.

As much as she'd enjoyed herself, she had to push the idea that there might ever, could ever be more out of her thinking. He was a musician and he'd be leaving. He didn't belong in Cedar Springs. Not long term, anyway. But did she?

The question was so unexpected and disturbing that she froze for a moment before she turned the water off and stood in the shower as the water dripped from her body. Did she belong in Cedar Springs? She'd always thought so. Even when she'd moved away to go to school and prove to herself and everyone else that she could be a single mom and raise Jules on her own, she'd always thought about coming back to her hometown. When the job at the Springs opened up, it was like a sign that she could have her career and raise her daughter in a small town. But did that mean she belonged there?

Now that her mother spent most of her time in Arizona, they only had friends to call family. And even though she had moments when it seemed as if she were settling in, it was no secret that Jules missed the city and the busier way of life.

She couldn't be serious. Was she seriously standing there, the memory of Slade's touch still fresh on her body, planning how she could possibly have a future with him? Beth reached up and wrung out her hair.

She was being more than ridiculous. She needed to stop thinking, and just enjoy herself. As she wrapped a towel around her now chilled body, that's exactly what she pledged to do.

No more thinking. At least not until later.

IT DIDN'T SEEM to matter that it had been months—heck, probably years—since Slade had the opportunity to cook breakfast, let alone for a beautiful woman. In fact, he couldn't seem to remember ever having that opportunity before. Nor had he wanted to. Beth brought out something completely different in him and as he puttered around the kitchen, opened cupboards and peered into the fridge, he decided he liked it. He liked it very much.

He'd hummed all morning, a tune that had worked its way into his head. If there'd been a guitar in the house, he would have picked it up and worked out the melody right then, but letting the lyrics and the general feeling of the song roll around in his head would have to do. It was Beth. She inspired something in him. Something great, and he was in no hurry to let it go. Or her.

Your touch, your breath on my skin.
When you say my name, I'm lost to you,
And you don't even know what you do.
Shatter me, baby. Shatter me.

The words slipped easily from his lips as he collected the ingredients for a simple omelet. With an extra flare, Slade cracked an egg against the counter and let it slip into the bowl using only one hand. He whirled around to find a whisk, and the words died on his lips when he saw Jules at the back door.

"Hey there, I'm—"

"In my house." She crossed her arms over her chest and leaned against the doorframe.

The cold air she'd let in when she came in hit him, and he glanced down at his naked chest. He hadn't even thought of a shirt. Hell, he'd barely thought of pants, especially considering his plan had been to serve Beth breakfast in the bedroom, where he could feast on her. He shook his head hard in an effort to clear all dirty thoughts from his mind because clearly that wouldn't be happening with Beth's daughter home. And her arrival brought a whole host of new problems. At least that's surely how Beth would see it.

"I am," he said after a minute. "Are you hungry?" Best to play it naturally, he decided. "I'm making breakfast."

"I can see that." She narrowed her eyes at him, but then to his relief, dropped her arms and shrugged out of her jacket. "I am hungry actually. Do you even know how to cook?"

Slade laughed and grabbed another egg from the carton. He cracked it easily, and drew out the motion for her benefit. "Obviously, I'm a pro."

Jules peeked into the bowl. "Except for the piece of shell." She grinned. "But yeah, otherwise, a total pro. Maybe it should be your new career."

He shook his head. The girl could definitely dish it out. If he didn't know better, he would have sworn she was older than twelve. She seemed so much older than her years. Not that he'd spent much time around kids at all except for the ones screaming at him for autographs. "A smart ass, hey?"

"A smart aleck." She emphasized the last word. "We don't swear in this house. Mom would lose it."

Slade nodded. "Gotcha. I wouldn't want to upset your mom."

"Trust me, you wouldn't."

Slade returned his focus to the eggs. He quickly cracked a few more into the bowl before he located a chopping board and got to work on the vegetables. He didn't feel right talking about Beth to Jules, especially as it was awkward enough for him to be in their kitchen in the morning. But if Jules thought it was awkward, she didn't say anything. Maybe she was too young to know what it meant. For Beth's sake, he hoped that was true. It would be hard enough to be a single mom without having to deal with situations like that. A totally irrational flare of jealousy flashed through him. Had Beth dealt with situations like this in the past? With who? Is that why Jules didn't seem too upset to see him there?

He chopped the onions with a bit more force than necessary at the thought of another man putting his hands on Beth.

"What did they do to you?"

"What?" He turned, the knife still in his hand.

Jules held up her hands. "The onions," she said. "What did they ever do to you? You're attacking them." She smiled and Slade could see the little girl she tried so hard to hide.

"Oh, right. I was just thinking about something." He chopped the vegetables and dumped them into his egg mixture. He needed to change the subject. "Did you have fun last night?" It was all he could think of. "It seems fun, living in a town that does things like that all the time."

"I guess."

He caught an undertone in her voice, but didn't turn around. "You don't like Cedar Springs? What about your friends?"

"They're alright, I guess. But they don't…"

"Don't what?" Slade poured some of his mixture into a hot pan before he finally turned to look at her. He didn't have any experience trying to get a pre-teen to open up about something that was clearly on her mind, and under normal circumstances, he probably wouldn't even try. But he was definitely not in a normal situation, and Jules wasn't normal, either. She was Beth's daughter. And dammed if that didn't make him care.

"They don't get it," Jules said after a moment. "Tori thinks that Cedar Springs is the best place on earth, and she's already talking about getting married and living here forever."

"And you don't want to do that?"

"Hell no!" Her hand flew to her mouth. "I mean, heck no." Slade swallowed his smile. "There's nothing happening here. Even the city isn't much better, but it's a start. I want to go to

Los Angeles, or New York, or Europe. Somewhere where things are happening."

There was so much enthusiasm behind her words, he couldn't help but get caught up in what she was saying. "What kinds of things do you want to happen?"

"Anything. Everything. I want to be somewhere where no one knows who I am. Where I can walk down the street and not have every single person know where I'm going and what I'm doing."

"That's the big city alright." Slade nodded. "The problem with that is, no one cares, either." He turned back to the omelet and deftly flipped it, secretly pleased with himself that he remembered how. "There's something to be said for having people care about you." He slid the omelet onto a plate and thought over what he'd just said.

There was something to be said for that. He'd been on the road for years. Traveled from one big city to the next and, even though he was recognized everywhere he went, no one knew him. And certainly no one cared. It was an empty life. And up until that moment, Slade hadn't realized just how empty it had been. Wasn't that the real reason he'd come back to Cedar Springs and the resort? The people here were real. They cared. Beth. She cared. He could feel it in the way she kissed him. There was so much they didn't know about each other, but it didn't matter.

"Is that for me?" Jules broke through his thoughts as she gestured towards the plate.

"Yes." He put it in front of her on the table and opened drawers until he found the cutlery and handed that to her as well. Still stunned from the revelation he'd made while standing in front of the stove, he poured himself a cup of coffee and took a moment to pull himself together before he prepped another omelet.

"Is that what you really think?" Jules asked with a mouthful of egg. "Or is that what you're telling me because you're an adult and you have to?"

"Nope," he said, meaning it. "It's true. Don't get me wrong. The world is a cool place, and I love to travel. In fact, I'd recommend it. One day you should absolutely get out there and see the world. But there's nothing like coming home."

Jules eyed him suspiciously. "But this isn't home for you. I thought you were from Toronto. And that's a big city, too."

"You've done your research." He winked at her and she blushed more like the teenage girls he was used to dealing with.

She shrugged and stuffed more eggs in her mouth. "Tori reads all those gossipy magazines."

"And they say I'm from Toronto?"

"Yup, and you were adopted and your parents died."

Her words should have hurt him, but she wasn't trying to be insensitive; she was just reciting the facts the magazine reported. Besides that, it was true and Slade had long ago gotten over feeling bad about what was his life. He'd been adopted as an infant to his parents, who'd met late in life and couldn't have children of their own. He grew up with everything he'd ever wanted, but he was only nineteen when both his parents passed on: his mom from a heart attack, his father less than a year later. He'd always assumed it was a broken heart.

"It's true," he said. "Tori has her facts straight. So I guess I don't really have a home anymore. But I like it here."

"You're crazy."

"No, really," he said, suddenly serious. "It feels like home here. Like I could be happy in a place like Cedar Springs."

Jules shook her head. "I still think you're nuts and I don't get it." Jules stared at him. Her eyes were so much like her mother's but different, too. Jules' eyes sparkled, as if she were ready for an adventure. "According to Tori, you joined up with the Jacked Crackers when you were older. What did you do before then?"

Slade ran a hand through his hair and took another deliberate sip of his coffee. He didn't remember a lot about those years, but that was because he'd hopped from one small town to another, caught a ride with whomever he could, drank his way through women and bars, and tried to write songs good enough to sell. Eventually he'd written the right song; Axel heard it and introduced him to the rest of the band. That's when everything changed. It wasn't a time Slade liked to remember.

"I guess I just traveled around," he said in way of explanation. "There was always someone willing to give me a ride to the next town and the next bar. All I wanted to do was play music."

"How did you get rides?"

Slade laughed. "Have you ever been to a greasy spoon gas station diner? There's always somebody who needs a little company. Rides weren't the problem."

"I guess it's a good way to travel."

"No." He laughed and returned his attention to the stove where he finished off the last omelet and slid it onto a plate, ready for Beth. "I wouldn't say that."

"Well, I guess you had to do what you had to do."

Slade nodded. "Are you sure you're only twelve?" He joined her at the table. "You seem pretty put together for a kid."

"I've gotta be." She wiped her mouth with the back of her hand. "It's always been just me and Mom."

He knew he shouldn't ask her, but he couldn't help it. "So, has it always been just the two of you?" he asked. "Or has there been—"

"Good morning. I thought you were at Tori's."

BETH HAD to wrap her arms around her chest to keep from shaking. She was sure they both could see it as they whirled around at the sound of her voice. What was she doing there? Jules was supposed to be at Tori's and instead she sat at the breakfast table with a half-naked rock star. The half-naked rock star her mother had just slept with. Repeatedly.

Oh God.

She took a deep breath and focused on exhaling slowly, giving her time to pull herself together.

"I was at Tori's," her daughter said. "But she had homework and her parents freaked out when they found out she barely passed the science test last week."

Beth nodded, not really hearing her. Her eyes focused on Slade, his bare chest. The smooth, sexy, hard chest she'd woken up on not too long ago. He jumped up from his seat and started towards her.

No. He couldn't do that. He couldn't come to her and kiss her and…no. Not in front of Jules. She glared at him, hoping to impress upon him that he needed to keep his distance.

"You're just in time." He stopped directly in front of her, and although he didn't kiss her, he took her hand and led her to the table where he sat her in the seat he'd just vacated. "Jules and I were just talking about—"

"I heard what you were talking about." She shot him another look, but his back was turned to her. "I don't think you need to press my daughter for information on my personal life." Her voice came out much harsher than she'd intended and when he turned to place a plate and cup of coffee in front of her, she didn't miss the flash of hurt on his face. Or maybe she'd imagined it, because when she looked again, it was gone, replaced by his smooth smile.

"He wasn't. We were just talking and Slade made me

breakfast." Jules held up her empty plate. "Tori is going to freak out when she hears you made me breakfast." Beth dropped her fork against her plate and Jules stared at her. "What? She cares about these things. I don't."

"I know." Beth forced her voice to sound as calm as possible. The last thing she needed was Tori's mom and everyone else in town knowing Slade was in her house early enough to cook anyone breakfast. "But I don't think we need to tell Tori that Slade was here." She flicked a glance in Slade's direction, but the sight of his grin had her looking away again. Apparently she wasn't going to be able to count on him for support in this. "Why don't you keep it between us for right now?"

"But, it's not a big deal." Jules looked between the two of them, and Beth prayed she was too young to put it together. Especially with Slade's shirtlessness. Her daughter was definitely more mature than Beth often gave her credit for but she was still so naive in some ways, and as far as Beth was concerned at that moment, that was fine with her.

"Your mom's right. Let's keep it our secret for now."

Jules' face fell.

"But why don't you go ahead and tell them I'll come by the school and play some songs for them?"

Beth whipped her head around in time to see Jules' face light up. For all her pre-teen attitude, Jules was still a kid and one who was obviously very excited to be responsible for bringing a private concert to her school.

"Really?"

Slade smiled. "Really. You clear it with your teacher and I'm there."

"Oh my God." Jules jumped up from her chair. "Tori is going to freak out. I have to go call her."

Seconds later, Jules had fled from the room, presumably to spread the word. "That was nice of you."

"It's no big deal." Slade shrugged, and Beth swallowed

hard at the sight of his rippling muscles. It was really ridiculous the effect he had on her. It was also dangerous. "Besides," he continued. "She's a good kid. I like her."

His words sparked something in her, but there was no way Beth would get excited just because he said he liked her kid. "You should put a shirt on." She looked away and took a deep drink of her coffee.

"You should eat something." He came to stand behind her; she could feel the heat of him through her sweater. "You worked up quite the appetite last night." Slade's hands rested on her shoulders, and her body reacted instantly with a thrill right to her core.

"That's presumptuous of you." She tried her best to sound indifferent, but she was pretty sure she didn't fool anyone, least of all Slade. He moved his fingers, kneaded into her tense muscles. Beth closed her eyes to soak up the sensations he caused in her. A low moan escaped her lips and shocked her back into the present and the fact that he still stood shirtless in her kitchen while her twelve-year-old daughter was in the other room.

It was one thing for her to give in to her desires for one night. It was a totally different thing for her to bring it home, into their house, for her impressionable daughter to experience. She shrugged out of Slade's grip and stood next to the table. She just stared at him, with his hard, beautiful body, remembered the way he made her feel, the way he touched her…No. Guilt flooded through her. What kind of mother was she? She was acting like a teenage groupie.

"You should go." She turned away so she wouldn't have to look in his eyes. Or was it because she was afraid her will would melt away if she looked at him, remembered him kissing her, moving inside her? She couldn't answer that. Not even to herself.

"Beth." Slade reached out and slowly turned her body so

he cradled her in his arms. With one hand, he traced the line of her jaw. His thumb came to rest on her lips. He parted them gently before he met her lips with his own in a kiss that was at the same time hot and sweet. When he pulled away, Beth's chest heaved against his. There was no doubt: he could stir her with the simplest of touches, softest kisses. "No regrets, okay?"

It was as if he could see right into her mind and every single thought she'd had since she'd walked into the kitchen and had the reality of her life smack her in the face. She shook her head. "I don't…" She couldn't finish the lie. She did have regrets. Not for the reasons he thought, but because the harder truth was, now that she'd allowed herself the luxury of one night with Slade, she knew it would never be enough. And that shattered her.

"You should go," she repeated. She squeezed her eyes closed against the burn of tears.

He didn't release her right away, and when Beth opened her eyes again, he stared directly at her, the intensity in his own eyes shadowed by something else she couldn't quite pinpoint.

"Slade," she tried again. "You should—"

"I'm not walking away from this."

Her breath hitched in her chest.

"I don't think you understand." He pulled her close, so she was pressed up against the length of him. "You." He kissed her forehead. "Me." His lips left a soft kiss on her neck. "This." He kissed her lips softly, gently sucked in her bottom lip before he pulled away to whisper, "I'm not going anywhere."

Chapter Eight

THE REST of the weekend went by uneventfully, and even when Sam called to press Beth on details of her night with Slade, she'd only given her best friend enough details to stop harassing her. The thing was, Beth couldn't tell even her best friend what had happened with Slade when she still couldn't process it herself.

After the unexpected breakfast with Jules on Saturday morning, Slade left and presumably went back to the Springs. For the rest of the day, she'd replayed every moment they had together, including the words he'd spoken before he left. He hadn't run off, the way she would have expected him to. Hell, he hadn't done anything the way she'd expected him to. So much for the rock star love 'em and leave 'em stereotype.

She'd driven herself crazy for the rest of the weekend, trying to figure out what she was going to do with the man she couldn't get out of her head. She'd even begged off the usual Sunday afternoon of drinks with her friends, because being around other people was the last thing she needed, not even her closest friends. Especially not her closest friends. She needed to figure things out before she said anything to them.

"Mom. Earth to Mom." Beth snapped her head up from the cup of coffee in her hand that she'd let get cold as she'd become lost in her thoughts once again. "I'm going to be late for school." Jules grabbed a banana from the fruit basket and the simple action snapped Beth out of her reverie.

"You need more breakfast than that." She abandoned her coffee and rummaged through the cupboard to produce a breakfast bar that was likely stale, but nutritionally it had to be better than only a banana. Or not. But she needed to make some sort of effort.

Jules eyed the breakfast bar suspiciously before she grabbed it and stuck it in her bag.

"What do you have in there?" Her daughter's bag bulged and looked to be weighting Jules down. "You couldn't possibly have had that much homework this weekend."

Jules hugged her bag to her chest and shook her head. "I have to bring props for a play we're doing in social studies. It's about the Constitution and we need some supplies. I told the kids I'd be in charge of the props."

Beth couldn't remember Jules mentioning anything about a play, but there was a lot she couldn't remember these days. Her brain was so preoccupied with Slade that she knew she was missing a lot of the details. It had to change. She needed to focus and be a good mom. And she would, as soon as he left town and moved on. The thought caused a physical pain in her chest, but Beth ignored it. She had to, because there was no way the situation would end any differently.

"Come on," she said. "I'll drop you off at school or we'll both be late."

BY THE TIME Beth got up to the Springs, and left her car in the staff parking lot, she was five minutes behind schedule, which meant there would be no time to stop in the staff room and grab a fresh coffee. It was probably a good thing, too, because she had no doubt Carmen and possibly Kari would both be waiting for her, ready to drill her with questions about Slade. Sam wasn't the only one she'd avoided all weekend. They'd all seen her with Slade at the skating party. And they'd all seen her leave. There was no doubt they were all bursting with questions for her.

She made her way as quickly through the back hallways as she could, and out into the main corridor where the sun filtered through the wall of glass windows. It warmed the space, and as always, Beth instantly relaxed just walking through the gorgeous hallway. She used the time to let the stress of everything go. She needed to focus on her work. She had no time for thoughts of Slade or—

Beth slammed into a hard wall of muscle and man, dazing her for a second.

"Are you okay?"

She looked up into Jax's handsome face. He was the head chef at the Springs restaurant, Stillwater, and although she didn't see much of him—he was always hiding in the kitchen— the little she knew about him, she liked. He was an easygoing guy, until it came to food. Then, there was nothing he was more passionate about.

"I'm so sorry, Beth. I wasn't looking where I was going." He clasped her arms, and gave them a quick squeeze before he released her. "I was just headed to Dylan's office. I need to...it doesn't matter." His smile stretched from ear to ear and gave him a boyish charm. "Are you okay?"

"I'm fine." She nodded. "I wasn't watching either. I'm running late. It seems to be a habit."

Jax laughed. "Well, I'm glad you're okay. I'll see you around, okay? And next time you want lunch, it's on me. Just pop in and say hi."

Beth smiled and promised she would before she jogged the

rest of the way to her therapy rooms. Her first client was Mona Sheridan and although she probably wouldn't be too worried if she was late, it would set her entire day behind schedule.

Before she walked into the room where Mona already waited for her, Beth grabbed the stack of files she'd need for the day and flipped through them. She had a new client on the schedule. A Simon. New clients were always exciting. As much as she enjoyed getting to know her patients, and looked forward to seeing them, Beth also enjoyed the challenge that a new client brought. Besides that, it would keep her mind off Slade if she was busy with work.

She took her files and with a quick knock on the door, entered the room where Mona waited for her. "Good morning. I'm so sorry I'm late. It's been one of those days already."

Mona waved away her apology. "I'm not worried. I have nowhere else to be."

It was refreshing to have such easygoing clients. The Springs wasn't only a high-quality resort; it attracted the highest quality of people. Beth smiled and got to work. "Did you soak in the pools all weekend?" She started a slow massage on Mona's legs. They felt looser, and more mobile. And there was no doubt in Beth's mind that the mineral waters did ease the pain of arthritis and improve mobility. She'd seen it time and time again, and she could tell before Mona spoke what the answer would be.

"I did," the other woman said. "In fact, I had a lovely weekend reading and soaking. I turned into a bit of a prune." She laughed. "But I feel so much better. Like I could go for a jog."

"Well, I don't know about that. But I'm glad you're feeling better. The springs really do help. If only we could bottle it so you could take it home with you."

Mona grew serious as Beth moved to the other leg. "I won't

be going home for a while," she said. "I just extended my stay by another month."

"A month?"

"Of course." Mona's mouth pressed into a line. "My granddaughter, Bria, isn't all that happy about it, but she doesn't understand what a difference being here has made to me. Do you have any idea what it's like to live in a constant state of pain?" Beth shook her head. She really had no idea. "Neither does my Bria, but let me tell you that when you're my age, and still feel like you have a lot of life left in you, but your body doesn't seem to agree, it gets a little depressing after awhile."

"I can imagine." Beth moved her fingers around Mona's calf muscle. "You're far too young to feel so limited by your body."

"Exactly. Which is why I'm staying. In the few weeks I've been here, I've seen such an improvement. Bria doesn't understand. She thinks you're all running a scam up here."

Beth's fingers froze. "What?"

"Don't pay her any mind." Mona waved her hand. "She's young and skeptical and far too cynical for her own good. But I'm not letting her feelings influence anything. I know what I know. And I know there's magic in those spring waters."

Beth smiled. There was magic in the water, alright. Her mind flew back to the first kiss she'd shared with Slade. Damn. She couldn't even get through one patient without thoughts of him. She was in for a long day.

"I see that smile," Mona said with a wink. "You're thinking of Simon, aren't you?"

Her whole body froze, except for her heart, which picked up its rhythm with an intense pounding. "What?" Beth's mind spun. Simon? That's what Mona had called Slade the other day when they'd run into him in the pools. "Who?"

"Simon." There was no missing the hint of a smile that

played on Mona's face. "Excessively handsome, smooth guitar player," she said. "You know, the one you couldn't take your eyes off of?"

Beth shook her head. "No, that's not—" But it was. A thrill ran through her at the thought that he'd gone to the effort of booking an appointment with her. When he hadn't called her all weekend, Beth started to play out a million scenarios in her head, all of which had ended with him leaving town without saying goodbye.

"Looks like your day is about to get a whole lot better." Mona winked at her and made googly eyes until Beth laughed along with her. She didn't know about better, but suddenly Beth knew her day was going to get a whole lot more interesting.

SLADE PACED the length of his suite, trying to ignore the nattering voice that came through the phone. He'd done his best to put Max off, even turned his phone off for the weekend so he could finish some songs. It wasn't hard. One night with Beth had inspired him enough to write three more songs, all of which he was intensely proud of. But just because he was proud of them, he didn't know whether or not he was ready to share them. The lyrics burst with emotion. His emotions. It wasn't something he'd done with his songs before. He'd always played it safe, skated along the surface of anything real. But with this collection, it was raw. It was Beth.

"Max," Slade finally interrupted. "Relax, okay? I told you I'd get you the songs and I will. I'm working here. It's not like I'm sitting around poolside every day." Although there had definitely been some fun thrown in, Max didn't need to know that.

"Give me something, Slade. You have to give me something."

"They're not ready." The lie rolled easily off his tongue. "I need more time."

"You're running out of time. I've kept the guys calm by telling them you're working on something great, but they want to hear it. They're getting nervous, Slade."

He walked to the window, but Slade didn't even see the mountains he stared out at. The songs were raw. They were edgy for the Jacked Crackers, totally unlike anything they'd ever done before. Slade honestly didn't know how the guys would react to them. And more than that, he didn't care. And wasn't that the real reason he was so hesitant to share? Slade knew the songs were good. Better than good; they were great. But they weren't Jacked Crackers material. They were Slade Black material.

"Give me another week."

"Slade, I can't—"

"I need another week, Max."

Maybe by then he could figure out what he was going to do.

His manager still talked; his voice grew louder, even as Slade took the phone away from his ear. He looked over at the clock on the nightstand. He didn't have time to deal with Max. He had an appointment to get to. Slade pushed the button on his phone, silenced his irate manager and tossed it on the bed before he grabbed his key card and headed down to the main hall of the Springs to meet his new physical therapist.

SLADE KNEW it was a bit risky to book an appointment with Beth. She probably had other patients who needed to see her, but dammit, he needed her more. And he couldn't wait all day to see her again and if it meant posing as a patient, then he was pretty sure he could use a little physiotherapy of his own. But he'd meant what he'd said in her kitchen the other day. Whatever it was between them, he wasn't going to just walk away. He'd never felt a connection quite like the one he did with Beth. Not even close. And he'd be dammed if he was going to sit back and let it slip away.

When he got to the therapy rooms, he checked in with the same man he'd seen at the desk a week ago—Josh, his name tag said. On an impulse, Slade had used his given name of Simon because it would be nice for someone to know the real him. Not the rock star. He waited in the chair and flipped through a magazine, not really seeing the images in front of him.

He knew the second she walked into the room. The hair on the back of his neck stood up and his whole body tensed with anticipation. Without looking up, he waited for her to call his name.

"Simon." She said his name with a smoothness, a familiarity that spoke to the night they'd spent together.

When he looked up and locked eyes with her, her expression was nothing but professional. The juxtaposition between the sides of her set him on fire. He got up from his chair and crossed the room in two steps to stand in front of her. "That's me." His voice was laced with promise, and he could barely restrain himself from reaching out and grabbing her delectable ass as she led him from the reception room to a small treatment room.

The moment they were inside and the door was closed, he reached for her, but she dodged him and deftly put a stool between them. Every instinct he had urged him to take her by the arm and pull her hard against his chest, kiss her until she begged for more. But he waited. Beth took her time and flipped through his chart. He'd used the bogus excuse he'd used earlier with her co-worker that he had a sore wrist from playing. When she looked up at him, he held out his arm and weakly flexed his wrist for her benefit.

She smiled and raised her eyebrows. "The chart says it's your left wrist that's bothering you."

Slade looked down at his right arm, still extended in her direction, and smiled wickedly. "Sometimes it's both."

"Right." She closed his file and gestured to the therapy bed. "Why don't I take a look?"

"Really?"

"Really, Mr. Black. Isn't that why you came in here today?" Her eyes challenged him, but there was a sparkle in them, too, and he was more than willing to play along.

He grinned and held out his wrist. The left wrist this time. "Absolutely," he said.

Beth put down the chart she held and took a step towards him before she gently cradled his hand in hers. Her thumbs moved in gentle circles along the sensitive skin on the inside of his wrist. Slade had to brace himself against the thrills that flew through his body at her touch.

"Does this hurt?"

He shook his head and Beth moved her fingers around to the top of his hand. "What about this?"

When he didn't answer right away, Beth stopped her fingers and looked up. "Mr. Black?" Her voice was all professionalism and seriousness, but her eyes gave her away. "Does it hurt when I touch you there?"

She spoke slowly, each word drawn out for maximum effect. And hell if they didn't have just the right effect. He couldn't do it anymore. He couldn't stand there with her hands on him but not really touching him. Quickly, before she realized his plan, he flipped his hand around, clasped both of hers together and pulled her against him before he crushed his lips down onto her perfect mouth. He kissed her thoroughly and completely, until he was sure she would drop the facade.

He didn't release her, but lifted his face so he could stare at her deliciously swollen lips. "You know damn well what your touch does to me." Her entire body quivered in his arms, and Slade kissed her again before he took a step back. It was one thing to book an appointment with her, but letting his hormones get the best of him at her place of employment was a step too far, even for him.

Beth turned away and picked up his folder again. He watched while she flipped it open and jotted something down, her back to him. After a moment, she closed it and faced him. A small smile played at her lips. "Well, Mr. Black, I think there's only one way to treat your symptoms."

Slade's body reacted without question to her words. "And what's that?"

"You should be soaking in the spring waters."

His excitement waned slightly, despite the idea of seeing Beth in her bathing suit again. "The pools?"

He couldn't miss the mischievous glint in her eyes. "Not just any pools," she said. "The natural pools. That is, if you're up for a bit of a trek?" Her eyes flared with the challenge, and Slade was definitely not backing down.

SLIGHTLY MORE THAN AN HOUR LATER, Slade wondered whether there really were natural pools. They were both bundled up in ski pants, parkas, knit caps, and gloves and had been trudging through the forest on snowshoes for the better part of sixty minutes, and as far as Slade could see, they were no closer to a hot pool of any kind.

"Okay," he called to Beth, who was slightly ahead of him on the trail. "I give up. You were just trying to teach me a lesson, weren't you?"

"I don't know what you're talking about." Beth didn't turn around, but kept her shockingly fast pace.

She knew damned well what he was talking about. In a spurt of energy, Slade ran as best as he could with his clumsy snowshoes on, and caught up to her. He grabbed her arm and together they fell into a heap in the soft snow. Slade used his arms to shelter her and rose above her. He stared down into her beautifully stunned face.

"What was that for?"

"You're tormenting me."

She laughed. "And what if I am?"

He slid one hand along the length of her, frustrated by the thick layer of clothing between them. "It's not nice to torment a frustrated man." Beneath him, her eyes darkened with desire and her tongue darted out to lick her lower lip. Slade barely restrained a groan. "You're killing me, Beth."

"Well, it's certainly not my intention to kill you, Mr. Black. After all, I am your physiotherapist and I'm—"

"So give me a little therapy."

She laughed again and pushed at him so he fell back, off her and into the snow. "That was the worst line I've ever heard." She pulled herself to her feet and brushed the snow off. "I promised you a soak, and that's exactly what you'll get." The sexy way she tilted her head and smiled at him was all he needed to get up and rejoin her on the path. "It's only a few more minutes."

He kept pace with her the rest of the way up the path and true to her word, a few minutes later they came across a small clearing. The steam was heavy in the air, and despite the cool winter day, it immediately felt a little warmer. He wasn't sure what he expected, but there were no obvious signs of a hot pool until Beth led them up a slight hill and there, hidden almost in plain sight, was a rocky pool.

"Wow."

"I know, right?" Beth unclipped her snowshoes and

propped them up against a boulder. "And it's really private. Not many people know about it."

"Especially if the only way up here is by snowshoe. The hike is enough to put anyone off."

She laughed.

"What?"

"There's a road, too." She pointed over her shoulder. "I just wanted to make you work for it. As part of your therapy, you know?"

He shook his head, but wasn't angry. He deserved it, and more for the way he'd weaseled his way in to see her. "So, if it's alright with my physiotherapist, can we get in and get wet?"

SHE KNEW it was kind of a mean thing to do to him, but it was fun, too, and she'd wanted to see if her rocker could handle a little outdoor excursion. She paused a bit at the thought that he was *her rocker* but she'd be dammed if she could think of him as anything but. And although it wasn't the best move to book in as a client and occupy her entire afternoon with a bogus ailment, it was also pretty sweet and it did give them the chance to spend some uninterrupted time together.

She moved quickly against the cold. Beth stripped out of her outer clothes and left them on a dry rock before she slipped out of her clothes and wrapped one of the towels she'd packed around her naked body. She hadn't bothered with a swimsuit, as she knew it would be secluded up in the forest. It wasn't a place they told the guests about, so she was confident that no one would bother them. When she was ready, Beth stepped towards the water and looked around for Slade.

Despite what they'd already shared together, she'd insisted on having him undress on the other side. It was silly, and she knew it, but she needed something, no matter how small, to keep a distance between them. Her feelings for him, and scarier still, the way he made her feel when she was with him, scared her. No matter how much she tried to tell herself that what happened between them was a one-time thing, she knew deep inside that wasn't true. And that terrified her.

"I'm over here." His voice came from the mist on the other side of the rocky pool. "You must be freezing. Get in here."

The fact that he could see her and not the other way around was exciting, and a shiver ran down her spine. Suddenly emboldened, she dropped her towel, and stretched her body before she carefully stepped down into the steamy water. The rocks were slippery and despite the fact that she tried her best to be sexy and seductive, her foot slipped on a stone. Beth would have gone head first under the water, but Slade was there, with one hand on her elbow, the other wrapped around her waist to steady her.

"Thank you, Mr.—"

He put a finger to her lip to silence her. "No more of that Mr. Black nonsense." Slade tightened his grip on her and pulled her around so the bare skin of her chest pressed up against his.

"That's usually how I address my patients." She knew she was being cocky, but she couldn't seem to stop herself.

"Okay. I give." His actions belied his words as he clearly wasn't giving physically. "But I'm not going to apologize for my fake appointment. I needed to see you, and it worked, didn't it?"

She grinned. "It did."

"Good." One hand lifted from the water and left droplets on her cheek. He gently raised her face so she looked up at him. "Because I don't think I could go one more day without this. I need you in my arms, Beth." He swallowed hard. "I need you."

His hardness pressed against her belly left no room to deny

what it was exactly that he needed from her, and by the tightness of her own body, the desire coiled deep in her core, it was exactly what she needed, too.

The heat of the water wrapped around them, but it was nothing compared to the heat between them as he kissed her and lifted her so she could wrap her legs around his waist. With Slade kissing her, touching her, needing her, all her worries, reasons for not being with him, arguments against what she was doing, everything…they all melted away because there was nothing more perfectly right than being with him in that moment.

He broke their kiss long enough to ask, "Are you on the Pill? Are you—"

"Yes." The word escaped her in a breath and before she could even get it out, he was inside her, filling her and making everything okay.

She clung to him, desperately trying to hold back her own climax, as his hands on her hips guided her in a frenzied rhythm. It felt like only seconds before she felt the tingling low in her belly that spread through her limbs, and threatened to shatter her completely. She bit down on his shoulder in an effort to muffle the climax that—

"Beth!"

The voice broke through her passion-clouded haze. It was close. Too close. Beth's eyes flew open as she pushed back and away from Slade. Instantly, the emptiness left behind consumed her, but she focused instead on the voice.

"Beth!"

Her eyes flew to Slade. He looked just as stunned as she felt but she didn't have time to think about it, let alone do anything about it, because moments later, Kari Fox's head appeared around the bend. Besides the fact that she'd been working at the Springs for a few months and dating one of Beth's best friends, she still hadn't had time to get to know Kari very well, and there was no reason that Kari should be seeking her out now, except…

"Kari?" Beth moved in the water, putting distance between her and Slade and also so Kari might be able to see her through the steam. "What's wrong?"

Kari squinted, as if trying to make out her figure through the haze. Beth saw the moment Kari realized Beth wasn't alone. Her eyes darted to the pile of clothes, to Beth and beyond, likely to Slade, before they landed on Beth once again. "I tried calling your cell but you didn't answer," she said, "and thankfully you left a note that you were headed up here, otherwise I wouldn't have known where to find you. But——"

"What's wrong?" Beth felt a chill go through her despite the heat of the water around her. "Kari. Tell me."

Kari's eyes settled on her. "It's Jules. She's missing." Beth's blood ran cold and she didn't hear the rest of what Kari said as a roaring filled her head.

Chapter Nine

SLADE TRIED to take Beth's hand in his and offer her some comfort, no matter how small, but she yanked her hand away from his. They were cramped in the front seat of the Springs' maintenance truck that Kari had borrowed to find Beth. He tried to sneak a glance over at her as they bumped down the snowy trail, back towards the resort, but her eyes were fixed straight ahead out the windshield.

Kari, whom he'd only met briefly a few days earlier, didn't say a word about finding the two of them the way she had. He didn't know whether she was a close friend of Beth's or not, but he hoped she would continue to be discreet about the situation. He made a mental note to talk to her as soon as they had a chance. Not that it was important at the moment. Beth's daughter was missing, and that was all that mattered.

"What did the school say?" Beth asked the question for what had to be at least the tenth time.

If Kari was sick of repeating it, she didn't show it. "They said she failed to show up for homeroom. They tried calling you to see if it was an excused absence; that's when they called the Springs. I told them you were with a client." Slade flinched at the word and reminded himself it wasn't the time.

"And you called Rhys?"

Kari nodded. "I did. I couldn't get a hold of you, and I knew he'd be able to swing by your house and check to see if Jules had gone home sick."

"Thank you."

Rhys and Beth were old friends, she'd told him as much, and when Slade had met him at the skating party, he seemed like a solid guy, and one who definitely cared about Beth and her daughter. And as one of the cops in town, Slade had no doubt he'd already put a call out for Jules. All while he was having sex with her mother in the woods. There was no doubt in his mind why Beth wouldn't look at him. If he felt guilty, he couldn't imagine what was going through Beth's head.

"He found a note in her room." Beth turned and stared at the other woman.

"A note?"

"Rhys said it didn't say much, just that she needed to see the world in order to live."

Slade felt as if he'd been punched in the gut. He'd said those exact words to Jules only days earlier. But he hadn't meant for her to go now. Not at twelve. Not without telling her mother. Heat flashed through him, and a bead of sweat tracked down his spine. What could he say? Where could a twelve-year-old get to? And how on earth would she get there?

"We'll find her," Slade said, lamely. He squeezed Beth's thigh. "Try not to worry." His words were weak, and thin even to his own ears. He'd done this. He'd caused this to happen.

Beth still didn't look at him, but it was the tear that slid down her cheek as she continued to stare out the windshield that broke his heart.

Moments later, they pulled up in front of the main doors. "I'm going to take her down to the Grizzly Paw," Kari said when Beth didn't move. "They've set up like a command center there." Beth made a small gasping noise and shook her head.

The thought of leaving her when she so clearly needed someone with her ripped at him, but Kari stared at him, trying to impart some sort of message with her eyes and when Beth wouldn't look up at him, he squeezed her leg again and whispered into her ear. "It'll be okay. We'll find her, Beth. I'll—"

"Just go." She said the words softly; her voice broke. With two simple words, the distance between them stretched.

"We have to get going." Kari looked at him almost apologetically. "We'll be at the Grizzly Paw."

Slade nodded and slid out of the cab of the truck. As they pulled away and headed down into town, Slade had never felt more useless than he did at that moment. And guilty.

There was no doubt in his mind that Jules was out there somewhere because of the conversation he'd had with her. Slade jammed his hands through his hair and tried to remember what he'd said. They'd talked about traveling, seeing the world, and…

His blood ran cold as the realization of what he'd said to Jules sank in. He knew where she was.

If it wasn't too late.

"I'M NOT GOING to say anything about—"

"Not now, Kari." Beth couldn't deal with thinking about Slade or what they'd been doing or any of the rest of it. Not while her daughter was missing and definitely not from Kari.

"I know," the other woman said. "I just wanted you to know that you don't have to worry. I mean, I won't say anything to anyone. And—"

"It's fine." Beth released a long sigh. "The only thing I'm

worried about right now is Jules. I'll worry about the rest of it all later."

Kari nodded and to Beth's relief focused on the road again. She would worry about Slade and the fact that she'd probably just lost her job as soon as she knew her daughter was safe, because that was the only thing that really mattered. She was a fool to think, even for a moment, that she could be the type of woman who could have an affair with someone like Slade Black and not have any repercussions from it.

And he'd left. He'd gotten out of the truck and left her alone. It didn't matter that she'd told him to go. In that instant, with him next to her, it was too much. Too raw. But she hadn't counted on the empty void that would be left once he did go. The second he'd slid away, she wanted to pull him back again. But she couldn't. That was over. Whatever it was with him, it had come to an end. It had to.

Her focus had to be on her daughter. That's where it should have been the entire time, but instead she'd been at the hot pools having—no. She wouldn't go there. She wouldn't let her brain go there even for a second.

Jules.

Not Slade.

That was her priority. It always had been. She'd simply allowed herself to forget for a little bit. No more.

The second Kari pulled the truck to a stop outside the Grizzly Paw, Beth hopped out and ran to the door. "Where is she?" Beth called out as soon as she burst through the doors. "Have you heard from her?"

Sam met her before she could take more than a few steps inside. Her friend grabbed her by the shoulders. "It's going to be fine." Sam stared directly into Beth's eyes and forced her to focus on something besides her growing hysteria. "Rhys is out right now looking for her. He's scanning the entire town. She couldn't have gotten far." Sam led her gently to the table closest to the bar. "Sit. I'll get you a coffee."

Beth closed her eyes and forced herself to take a deep breath, focusing on counting to ten as she exhaled.

"Hey kiddo." Her eyes flew open to see Archer, the head cook at the Grizzly Paw and one of her closest friends. Archer had always been more of a big brother to both her and Sam, and just seeing him made her feel better. She jumped up and let him hug her with his strong arms. "She's a good kid." He rubbed her back. "She'll be fine."

Beth pulled away and sank into the chair once again. "How do you know that?"

"I just know." Archer slid into the seat across from her as Sam returned with the coffee and joined them. Kari came inside and pulled up a chair. "You're not really going to make her drink that, are you?" Archer gestured to the steaming mug in front of Beth.

"She needs to warm up."

"Not with that." Archer stood and swept away the mug. "I love you, Sammie, but you're not known for your coffee. Well, maybe you are but not in a good way."

Despite herself, Beth smiled. Her friends were predictable in their banter, and there was comfort in that when she felt everything else slipping out of control.

"I'll make a fresh pot." Archer disappeared into the kitchen.

Sam simply shook her head before she turned her attention back to Beth. "Rhys said he'd call as soon as they found anything. He has guys all over this. Jules won't get far."

"But why would she…" She couldn't finish the sentence. Tears slid from her eyes and spilled down her cheeks.

"Why would she run away?" Sam asked. "It's not like her."

"I don't know." A flash of Jules and Slade in the kitchen together went through her head. Could it be because of Slade?

Was Jules upset that her mom had a man in the house? Beth shook her head, trying desperately to process the thoughts that swirled through her brain. That couldn't be it, could it? She'd seemed totally okay with everything. She wasn't upset, she was…

"Beth?" Sam placed her hand on her arm. "What? What is it?"

She swiped at her tears. "It's nothing. I was just thinking." Her eyes darted to Kari, who sat silently. She gave Beth a small smile of support. Beth still couldn't be sure that Kari wouldn't say anything about how she found them, but she couldn't be sure and even if Kari kept her word—Beth wasn't naive enough to think it wouldn't get out.

The phone rang, and all three women jumped up from the table. "I'll get it." Sam rushed to the counter and snatched up the phone.

Beth stared at her, tried to figure out who was on the other line and what they were saying.

"Yes," Sam said. "This is…right. Yes, the soup today is broccoli cheddar." Her friend rolled her eyes and Beth looked away with a sigh.

"Rhys said he would phone right away as soon as they know anything," Kari said.

"I know." Beth nodded. "That's the whole problem. Why isn't he calling?"

Kari reached out and squeezed Beth's hand. "He'll call."

SLADE DIDN'T HAVE much time to waste. If Jules had followed his advice, or non-advice, or whatever it was he'd said to her, she was probably at a greasy spoon diner on the highway somewhere, trying to get a ride. God help him if she managed to find one. A twelve-year-old girl had no place picking up rides on the highway from random truckers. Hell, nobody did. But especially not Jules.

As soon as he'd made the connection, Slade ran into the main lobby of the Springs and up to the front desk. A woman he'd never met worked the desk. "I need to speak to Trent or Dylan Harrison right away," he said. He knew he was rude, but he didn't have time for niceties. "It's an emergency."

"I'm sorry, Mr. Black," the girl said. "Neither of them is in right now. Is there some—"

"Where are they?"

"I'm afraid I'm not at—"

"Never mind." He looked around the lobby frantically, not sure what he was looking for. "I need a car." He turned back to the girl, who seemed to shrink into herself. "Where can I get a car?"

"I don't have—"

Slade slammed his fist on the counter. "Dammit. I need a car, now."

"Hey, is there something I can help with here?" A man wearing a work shirt, embroidered with the Springs logo, and a tool belt around his waist, approached the desk. "Is something wrong?"

"I need a car," Slade demanded. "It's an emergency, and I have to get down the mountain right away."

"Okay."

"Okay?" Slade hadn't imagined it would be quite that easy.

"Yes. Come with me." The man turned and walked away. Slade caught up with him and fell into step beside him. "Name's Kurt. I'm in charge of maintenance around here. I'll lend you my truck."

"You will?"

"Don't sound so surprised." There was just a touch of laughter in the other man's voice, which only confused Slade more. He wasn't about to look a gift horse in the mouth, but at the same time, he had a hard time believing a complete stranger would help him out. "Look." Kurt came to a stop and faced Slade. "I know who you are, I know Trent and Dylan like you, and more importantly, Beth's my friend and I'm going to assume this has something to do with her."

"How did...how..."

"It's a small town." Kurt reached in his pocket and drew out a set of keys that he handed to Slade. "Word gets around. Just promise me you won't wreck my truck."

Slade managed a small smile. "I won't."

"Good. It's the red beater out the staff doors." Kurt pointed to a door at the end of the corridor. "Just return it when you're done. And whatever you do, don't hurt Beth, okay?"

He was so preoccupied with getting the truck and going to find Jules, Kurt's comment took him off guard. "What? I won't—"

Kurt held up his hand. "Just don't. She's a good girl, man. That's all I'm going to say. Don't hurt her."

Slade took the keys and turned to leave, but before he did, he surprised himself by saying, "I don't intend to."

THE ROADS WERE a lot clearer than they were the last time Slade had tried to negotiate his way down the mountain, and he made it into town in record time. He steered the truck directly towards the highway. Slade had no idea where the nearest roadside diner might be, but he needed to trust his instincts, and his instincts told him there would be one fairly close. And since Cedar Springs wasn't a pass-through type of town, he banked on the idea that Jules had somehow managed to get herself out to the main highway.

Taking a chance, he turned west, pressed down on the accelerator, and pushed the old truck to the max. Soon enough he was rewarded with a roadside sign for Del's Diner.

"Jackpot."

He took the off-ramp at top speed and skidded into the parking lot. He screeched to a stop in front of the glass doors. Only a few trucks were parked in the lot, and Slade hoped that meant Jules hadn't managed to find a ride yet due to slim pickings. He flung open the door with such force it slammed against the doorjamb. The bells that announced his arrival crashed to the ground.

Slade ignored them, and the waitress who tried to greet him. "Jules!" He stormed through the restaurant and scanned the booths and tables for a young girl. "Jules!"

Heads turned to look at him, but none of them belonged to a twelve-year-old girl. Maybe he'd been wrong. Or maybe he was too late? No. He wouldn't let his mind go there. He wouldn't even consider the idea. Desperation welled up inside him. Slade spun and saw the waitress watched him.

With her hands on her hips, and her wrinkly mouth pressed into a tight line, she gestured with her head to her left and raised her eyebrows. A rush of air escaped his lungs and he mouthed a quick thank-you before he sprung around a table and past a partitioned wall, to the far side of the diner. Jules.

She was pushed up into the corner of a booth, her back to him. She hugged her bag tightly to her chest.

"Jules." Slade slid across the vinyl seat so he sat directly next to her. "Are you okay?"

Her eyes, wide with fear and stubbornness, turned to him. She nodded slightly and her lower lip quivered before she bit it. Slade wrapped an arm around her and pulled her close. "It's okay. You're safe."

"WE'VE CHECKED the bus stop, the high school, the community center, and all her friend's houses." Rhys stood in front of Beth and recited the list of places he'd looked and not found her daughter.

"Keep looking, Rhys."

"I am, Beth." He knelt in front of her, and stared into her eyes. He was a good friend and there was nothing but honesty and kindness on his face. "I promise you, we'll find her. I've just sent an officer out to the highway. I don't think she would have…"

The tears she'd managed to stem fell once again at the thought that her little girl had somehow managed to make it out to the highway on her own and might be even farther.

"I just don't understand," Sam said for the dozenth time after Rhys excused himself to continue the search. "Why would Jules…what was she…"

"Slade." The name came out like a whisper, but her best friend caught it. It was the only thing she could think of, the only possible explanation Jules would have for leaving so suddenly. It was Slade. It was her relationship with Slade. The thought cut her deep. Jules had always come first. Always. She'd never dated, and certainly never brought anyone to their house. Until Slade. And he wasn't just some random guy either, as much as she tried to pretend otherwise. She liked him. Really liked him. But if liking him, if liking any guy was going to cause her daughter to run away, it wasn't worth it.

Nothing was.

"Slade? Do you want me to call him?"

Beth shook her head, and wrapped her arms around her waist to keep herself from falling apart.

"Wait. You don't think Slade is responsible for…I don't get it, Beth." Sam's face wrinkled with confusion. "What does he have to do with any of this?"

Beth took a deep breath and exhaled slowly, giving herself

time to compose herself. "Slade." She forced herself to say his name. "He…"

"He's here."

Sam jumped up from her chair, right as the door opened and Slade, followed by Jules, who was tucked under his arm like a broken little bird, walked into the Grizzly Paw. Beth flew across the room. She tugged her daughter into her arms and squeezed her tight.

"Jules. Thank God you're okay." She kissed the top of her daughter's head, inhaling the sweet smell of her shampoo. "Where have you been? Are you okay? Where were you? Why would you…Oh my goodness, I'm just so glad you're okay." As she hugged her close, she realized that her little girl was almost as tall as she was. She rested her head on top of Jules' and opened her eyes to see Slade.

He stood with a cautious smile on his face, his arms crossed over his chest.

"You found her?"

He nodded in response to her question.

"Where?"

"Jules?" Sam stood next to them, her arm out. "Why don't you come sit down, kiddo? You're probably hungry."

Beth reluctantly let go of her daughter and Jules nodded before she gave her mother a small smile. "I'm sorry, Mom."

"It's okay, kiddo. Go with Auntie Sam and get Archer to make you a big burger."

Jules nodded and hand in hand with Sam, went to sit at the table Beth had just vacated. Reluctant to take her eyes off her daughter again, Beth repeated her question. "Where did you find her?"

Slade hesitated a moment. "At the diner on the highway."

"The highway?" Beth's hand flew to her chest. "How did she…"

"She got a ride from one of your neighbors," Slade said

quickly. "Don't be too hard on her. She lied to the neighbor and said you were meeting her there to go into the city."

"She lied?" Beth shook her head, trying to wrap her head around everything. "But why? I don't…"

"She wanted to get to the diner so she could hitchhike somewhere and see the world."

"That's the craziest thing I've ever heard. Why would she…" Beth trailed off because she could see the truth in Slade's eyes. Jules got the idea from him. That's why he knew where to find her. He'd given her daughter the idea to run away. Anger flared through her. She clenched her fists at her sides. "Get out."

"Beth, I didn't—"

"Get out," she repeated through clenched teeth. "I knew you were nothing but bad news. I knew nothing could be real with you. You're just a goddamned rock star who doesn't know the first thing about family or responsibility and what do you care anyway?" Beth knew she was yelling and that everyone in the pub would be staring at her, but she didn't care. Her emotions raw, she couldn't stop herself. "As soon as you're finished here, and have had enough of whatever it is you came to Cedar Springs for, you're just going to turn around and leave without any thought to who you're leaving behind or the mess you made." Tears blurred her eyes and she slammed her fists into Slade's unmoving chest. "Get out. Just get away from me. I can't do this. I just. Can't. Do. This."

He didn't move as she repeatedly pounded her fists into him, sobbing and incoherent. Beth didn't even register it when Archer came up behind her, grabbed her by the waist, and pulled her away from Slade. She turned in to his arms, and cried until she'd exhausted herself. When finally she opened her eyes again, Slade was gone.

Chapter Ten

BETH COULDN'T WAIT to get Jules safely home and tucked into her own bed, and that's just what she did after she finished eating and Rhys was done questioning her. Beth still couldn't believe Jules had been foolish enough to try to hitchhike her way out of town, and all because of some ridiculous story Slade had told her about when he was younger.

Damn him. She couldn't even count how many times that exact thought had gone through her head since he'd returned her daughter to her and she'd learned the truth. What had he been thinking? Whatever it was, it wasn't responsible or reasonable or in the least bit appropriate for a child. He was inappropriate for a child and totally wrong for her. Now more than ever, that was clear.

Beth closed the door to Jules' room and made her way out to her living room and the glass of wine she had waiting for her. If it took a major scare for her to finally get Slade out of her head, then that's what it took because she was done with him. She would never again allow someone so reckless to put her child in danger. It all came down to what was important. And that was Jules.

"Is she asleep?" Sam handed her a glass of wine and together they sat down in the living room. Beth wasn't ready to be on her own, not after such an emotionally charged day. Sam knew it without even asking and invited herself over. That's what made her such an awesome friend. And that's exactly what Beth needed.

"She is. Thankfully." Beth took a sip of her wine. "I think she was exhausted by her little adventure and more than a little embarrassed. For how grown up Jules likes to pretend to be, she's still a little girl."

"I think sometimes we all have trouble remembering that."

Sam was right. It was far too easy to think of Jules as a teenager, and at times, even a responsible teenager. But she still needed her mother, that much was clear after today. And Beth couldn't be there for her daughter if she was mixed up with Slade. Hadn't she demonstrated that by frolicking around with him in the natural pools while her daughter was basically trying to skip town? She hung her head and used her free hand to massage the knot at the base of her neck. No more. She was done.

"So, when are you going to tell me what's going on with you and Slade?"

Beth looked up to see her friend's knowing look.

There was absolutely no point in denying anything, and Beth knew it. Not when everyone saw her melt down earlier at the Paw. In fact, she was surprised it had taken Sam so long to ask. It wasn't like her to give Beth space on such a potentially juicy topic. Especially when she seemed to be hellbent on pairing her up ever since she found love with Trent.

"There's nothing going on."

"Because I'm stupid?" Sam tilted her head and gave Beth a look that she recognized as her "don't mess with me" look.

Beth pretended to examine her wine glass before she answered. "Fine. There's nothing going on now." She emphasized the last word. "Or ever again. It's just not going to work."

"Back up." Sam sat up straight in her seat. "Start at the beginning. I need to know how you got here." Beth sighed. The last thing she wanted to do was rehash everything between her and Slade. But maybe going through it with Sam would help. It certainly couldn't hurt. She was confused and twisted around with her feelings as it was. It couldn't get any worse.

"We hooked up."

"Yeah, I got that." Sam smiled and winked. "But I know you well enough to know there's more to it than that. A lot more. And really, I don't think in all the time I've known you, I've ever seen you go off on a guy the way you did with Slade earlier."

Beth shook her head. It hadn't been her finest moment, that was for sure. But she was scared. More than scared. She'd never felt like that in her whole life. "It was too much." She told Sam the truth. "Thinking Jules was gone, or in danger… I've never felt like that before, Sam. And when Slade brought her back…" She put her glass down and clutched a throw pillow to her chest.

"That's just it, Beth." Sam put her wine glass down and moved closer to her. "Slade brought her back to you, and you totally lost it on him. It wasn't his fault. He didn't do anything wrong; he brought—"

"You don't get it."

"Then tell me."

"He's no good for us. For me. He's a musician and…I can't fall for someone like him."

"Like him?"

"It's too different." She whispered the words, confessing for the first time. "I need to be a mom and he's…he's just…" She drifted off, trying to sort out what she was really feeling.

"Beth?" Sam prodded gently.

"He's dangerous."

Sam raised an eyebrow. "How exactly is Slade dangerous?"

"He's a rock star, for God's sake! His whole life is rock and roll, nightclubs, partying…he put those crazy ideas in Jules' head about traveling and…"

"And?"

"I'm scared."

"Of what?"

"Of feeling the way he makes me feel." Beth yelled the words and immediately clamped a hand over her mouth. She dropped her gaze and shook her head. No. It wasn't that. It wasn't her feelings for Slade she was afraid of. Was it? "I can't fall for someone like him."

"Beth?" Sam's voice was softer, concerned. Beth felt her friend's hand on her knee. "It's okay."

"No." She looked at her friend through a veil of tears. "It's far from okay because it doesn't matter how I feel about him, Sam. It won't work. It can't."

"It can."

Beth laughed, a hollow, tinny sound. "How?"

She didn't wait for Sam to try to convince her otherwise. There was no point, and more than that, Beth couldn't stand one more minute of thinking about Slade. It was over. After the emotional upheaval of the day, it was clear more than ever that whatever fun she'd been having with Slade needed to come to an end. She'd risked too much. And for what?

The last thing she wanted to see was the sad way her best friend looked at her, but when Beth opened her eyes, that's all she saw. The problem was that Sam had no idea what it was like to give up your whole life for a child. She had no idea what it was like to sacrifice everything because the minute you gave birth, it was as if a part of you was forever outside of your own body. And you'd do anything to protect that part, even if it meant giving up your own happiness.

"Forget it, Sam." Beth exhaled loud and long and reached for her glass of wine. "It was fun for a while though, and that's all it was ever supposed to be. Fun." She took a deep drink of her wine to swallow the lie on her tongue.

Maybe if she kept telling herself it was nothing more than a fling, she'd start to believe it.

AFTER BETH EXPLODED on him at the Grizzly Paw, Slade had slipped quietly out of the pub and walked through the streets of Cedar Springs to clear his head. He'd walked straight past Dream Puffs; even the delicious aroma of freshly baked cinnamon buns couldn't lure him through the door. He replayed every word Beth had screamed at him, remembered the hard slam of each fist as it collided with his chest. She'd needed to work out some emotions, that much was clear. But her words...had she really meant them?

That was the question that echoed through his head, long after he'd circled past her small house, stopped twice to stare at the darkened windows and remembered what it had been like to be inside with her. Being with Beth in her tiny bedroom, with the homemade quilt pulled over her naked body while she curled up next to him, had been a memory he wouldn't soon forget. And later, cooking breakfast for her and her daughter, the banter back and forth almost as if he...what? Belonged there? The idea was ludicrous.

He belonged on a stage in some city with thousands of fans screaming his name while he closed his eyes, let his music take him away, and forgot everything that was real. That was his life. Beth was right; he was going to leave Cedar Springs. He scrubbed his gloved hand over his face. He had no business there, in her life, in her bed.

He turned to walk away, back to the main street and the

truck he'd promised to return, but took one last look at the small house before he did. He'd hurt her, and the memory of her hurt cracked him inside. He wouldn't do it again. Besides, she was right. This wasn't his life. *Even if you want it to be.* The thought blindsided him, but he forced it away and walked back to the truck.

When he finally returned the truck to Kurt, the other man greeted him with a handshake and a slap on the back. "I heard what you did," Kurt said. "You're a real hero, finding Jules like that. Next thing you know, Rhys is going to recruit you for the force. Can you imagine that? A rock star cop?" He laughed, and Slade tried to join in, but couldn't seem to muster the energy. "I'm sure they'll throw a party for you at the very least," Kurt continued. "If there's one thing this town likes, it's a party."

Slade nodded and tried to make his escape. "That would be good, but I'll probably have to get going soon. The band's waiting on me." He hadn't even realized that would be his choice until he said it out loud. But it wasn't as if he had a choice, really. Staying wasn't an option, no matter how badly every fiber in his body yearned to stay. The pull to stay in Cedar Springs was almost a physical ache, but that didn't matter. It couldn't. "Thanks again," he said to Kurt before he excused himself.

Never before had Slade felt so emotionally wrung out. From the high of being with Beth in the pools to the honest terror he'd experienced thinking something might have happened to her daughter. Then the relief of finding her, only to be followed by a pain so deep at Beth's rejection, he physically hurt. The only thing he wanted to do was sneak up to his room, make the necessary call and leave.

He needed distance. What he didn't need was Mona Sheridan, as sweet as she was, to come around the corner and spot him at that moment.

"Simon," she called. "Simon Black. Don't think I don't see you over there."

There was pretty much no way he could get away without being spectacularly rude, so he forced what he hoped wasn't a totally fake smile on his face and turned around. "Mona. How's my favorite knitter doing?"

She blushed and brushed off his compliment. "I actually made you some mittens." She came to a slow stop in front of him. "I thought you might want to keep your hands warm, what with your sore wrist and all." She winked and Slade couldn't help but laugh.

"Good point, and I do appreciate it. But I don't think I'll need the mittens much longer."

"You're not leaving, are you?" The look of concern on her face was genuine, and Slade felt a twinge of guilt, which was ridiculous. Cedar Springs was not his home and it's not as if he could live in a resort for the rest of his life. No, a little voice in his head said, you can live in that cozy little house just off Main Street.

Slade shook his head hard to clear the voice and the idea that continued to plague him.

"Is something wrong, my dear?" Mona's face was lined with worry. "You look like you're thinking too hard and the only remedy I know for that is soup."

"Soup?" He blinked, caught off guard.

"Yes." Mona threaded her arm through his and led him in the direction of the dining room. "And since I don't have a kitchen here, we'll have to make do with whatever soup that handsome chef has whipped up today. Don't think I haven't had my eye on him."

"Really?" Slade tried not to laugh as he let the older lady lead him towards Stillwater.

"I may be old, but I'm not dead, young man. And considering you're so obviously spoken for, I've had to set my sights a little farther afield."

"Well, I don't know him, but Jax seems like a good choice," Slade said as they reached the restaurant. "But I'm hardly spoken for."

The hostess seated them right away, greeting Mona with a warm smile. She'd obviously endeared herself to the staff, and Slade was impressed when the hostess told them that Jax would be right out to see them.

Slade raised his eyebrows in question but Mona just smiled. "What can I say? I made him some mittens."

He shook his head and laughed as the hostess left to get their drinks and presumably the chef.

After she left, Mona didn't waste any time getting to the point. "Am I to assume that the reason for the long look on that handsome face of yours is due to a particular young lady and the fact that you don't think you're spoken for? Because it's too late. I've moved on."

She winked and Slade smiled. It was hard to hang on to his depressed mood around Mona. "You seem different, Mona. Feistier or something…feeling better?"

"Well, I can't sit around and feel sorry for my old body, now, can I? Besides, I am feeling better. A lot better. This place works miracles and that girl has magic fingers on my old arthritis. And since I'm feeling so good, I figured the least I can do is help you."

He was about to protest that he didn't need help, but they both knew it was a lie. But he didn't want to talk about Beth or the physical pain in his gut every time he thought about her. Or did he? Something about Mona made it easy for him to talk. Slade was just about to spill everything when a man in chef whites approached the table.

"You must be Jax." Slade extended his hand.

"The one and only." He shook Slade's hand with a firm

grip. "You must be Slade. I recognize you from your pictures." Slade laughed and took an instant liking to the chef, especially when he turned to Mona and said, "And I hear you've been harassing my staff again."

Mona blushed like a schoolgirl. "I was hardly harassing them. But I know what I want and I want—"

"Soup," Slade interjected. "We need soup."

Mona nodded. "We do. What's the special today?"

"For you? A delicious saffron-infused lobster bisque."

"We'll take two." Mona held up two fingers and Slade decided it probably wasn't a good time to tell her that he wasn't very hungry. "And a basket of that fresh bread, too," she added.

"Of course." Jax bowed dramatically. "Coming right up." Before he could turn and head back to the kitchen, Jax turned his attention to Slade again. "I heard what happened today, man. Good work with Jules. She's a good kid."

"You know Jules?"

"Of course. Beth's kid worked up here a bit this spring when the hotel opened up. She's something else, isn't she?"

"She is." Slade nodded thoughtfully, remembering the conversations he'd had with her. "Just like her mother." The last part slipped out, and he didn't realize he'd spoken aloud until he saw both Jax and Mona stare at him.

"Right." A grin played on Jax's face. "Well, word travels fast around here and I heard it was pretty cool what you did, finding her like that."

It was easy considering I gave her the idea to go there, Slade thought but didn't say. Instead, he nodded and spun the salt shaker around on the tablecloth until Jax excused himself to the kitchen.

"Ready to talk?"

Slade shook his head.

"You like her."

It wasn't a question, but Slade nodded anyway.

"And she likes you." Her voice was kind, like his mom's used to be.

Slade shrugged and still wouldn't make eye contact. He'd certainly thought Beth liked him and had he been asked that question a few hours ago, there would have been no question. But after the way she'd yelled at him...

"So what I don't understand is why you look like your dog just ran away. What's the holdup here?"

There was no way he was going to get into a deep conversation with Mona, no matter how kind and sweet she was. Slade decided to take the easy way out. "No holdup." He looked up and forced his voice to sound as relaxed as possible. "I'm leaving soon. The band's waiting for me. I was actually just about to go upstairs and call my manager to make the arrangements. Should be gone by tomorrow."

"Tomorrow?"

"Yup." He gave the salt shaker one final violent spin; it fell over and spilled on the tablecloth. He ignored it. "It's time to go. I'm done here. I wrote my songs. There's nothing left for me here."

Without a word about the salt, Mona scooped it up and tossed it over her shoulder before she dusted her hands together. She folded her hands on the table in front of her and watched Slade without saying a word.

When a few minutes had passed and she still hadn't said anything, Slade started to squirm and look around. Where was Jax with the dammed soup? How long did it take to put soup in a bowl anyway? Finally, with an audible sigh, he reached forward, took a pinch of salt and threw it over both his shoulders for good measure. "There. Happy?"

"Are you?"

"No," he shot back. "I mean, yes. Of course."

"Which is it?"

He weighed his options for a moment, but again decided against the truth. "Of course I'm happy. I have everything I want. Everything I've ever wanted." The lie was sour in his mouth. All he ever wanted was represented by Cedar Springs. And Beth. He'd known that from the first time he set foot in the town and laid eyes on her sweet—

"Dinner is served."

Slade sat back in his seat with a start as Jax placed a bowl of steaming soup down in front of each of them.

"Thank you, Jax. You are an absolute doll." She turned her smile to him. "If I was only a little bit younger—"

"Ssh." Jax placed a finger in front of his lips and winked at her dramatically. "Don't ruin what we have now." He waved his hands in a dramatic pantomime and backed away from the table. "Bon appétit."

As a matter of principle, Slade wasn't going to eat. But the second the rich aroma hit him, his stubbornness melted away. Without a word to Mona, he dug in, and to his surprise, enjoyed every bite of the meal.

"Thank you for dinner," he said when he had finished. He wiped his mouth with his napkin and dropped it on top of the empty bowl. "I should go. I have a phone call to make."

"Simon." She reached out and grabbed his hand. "I wasn't trying to be hard on you."

"No." He shook his head. "It's fine."

She continued as if she hadn't heard him. "Sometimes you need to take a good long look at what it is you think you want and what it is that you need. And then you have to get out of your own way."

He let her words sink in.

She patted his hand, and before she released him, she added, "I'll make sure you get those mittens."

Chapter Eleven

THE MORNING DAWNED BRIGHT; the sun glittered off the snow in a way that made it look as if it would be a warm day. Beth knew better, and it wasn't just because the floor was cold on her bare feet. A bright, sunny day in January almost always meant it was a very, very cold day in January. One look at the thermometer she had fastened to her kitchen window confirmed it: negative thirty degrees Celsius. If she didn't have to go to work and send Jules to school, she would've happily returned to bed, pulled the covers over her head and hibernated for the day.

But there was no doubt her job was on the line, and after talking to Jules the night before, Beth didn't really think there was a risk of her running again. It was a poor decision, that was all. And probably one of many to come, Beth thought with a sigh as she set the coffee maker. It was only just beginning as Jules got closer to those teenage years. What had her father always said? Something about even the smartest kids shutting their brains off until they turned twenty-one. Beth shook her head at the thought and laughed.

"What's so funny?"

Jules stood in the entry to the kitchen, an oversized hoodie pulled over her pajamas. She looked so much like a little girl with her ponytail sticking out and sleep still in her eyes that Beth had to resist the urge to pull her close. Jules was growing up; she needed to remember that. "Good morning, kiddo. You have a good sleep?"

Jules nodded and shuffled to the table, where she slumped into a chair. "What were you laughing at?"

"Just something your grandpa used to say, that's all." She pulled the pot of coffee out and quickly poured herself a cup before it finished brewing. "Are you ready for school today?"

"I'm not going to do it again, Mom. I said I was sorry."

Beth sat across from her daughter. "I know. I wasn't trying to say that you would." She looked right into Jules' eyes, so much like her own, and smiled. "I trust you, Jules. But we're a team, and we need to be able to talk about things, okay?"

Jules nodded and picked at a string on her sleeve.

She knew it was early in the morning to push, but Beth still needed a few answers. Treading carefully, she said, "You do know that there will be lots of time for traveling when you're older, right? When you finish school, you can go out and see the world."

"You didn't."

Her words cut deep. No. Beth hadn't traveled. But she also hadn't planned to get pregnant so young and raise a child on her own. "No," she said. "I didn't. But there's time. I will."

"When?"

"I don't know, kiddo. Later."

When would she travel? It wasn't something she'd given much thought over the years. *Except for the last few weeks.* A voice piped up in the back of her head. Hadn't it been true that she'd thought of seeing the world? Contemplated what it could be like to travel, to be on tour? Beth shook her head and stood from the table. It was a childish dream, and one she should stop thinking about. Needed to stop thinking about.

"How about toast this morning?" She forced cheerfulness into her voice despite the sudden urge to sob.

"Sure."

Beth set about preparing breakfast and trying to reset her mind. She'd spent the entire night trying to get Slade off her mind and to reprogram herself to stop thinking about what was never going to be. Maybe if she was a different person, living a different type of life. But she wasn't. And the sooner she let that go, the sooner she'd be okay.

"Here you go." She put the toast in front of Jules, along with the peanut butter and a jar of jam. She watched while her daughter moved in slow motion to butter her bread. "You're okay, right, kiddo? I mean, we're okay? After everything?" Jules blinked and took a bite of her toast, so Beth kept talking. "We're a team, you and me. Just us against the world." She forced a smile she didn't totally feel and looked down into her coffee cup.

"But why does it have to be just us?"

Jules' question startled her and she looked up so quickly Beth sloshed her coffee onto the table.

"What?"

"Why does it have to be just us?" Jules repeated. "I mean, why can't there be someone else?"

Beth's breath hitched in her chest and she forced herself to take a deep breath before she asked, "Like who?" Jules shrugged and looked away, but Beth wasn't fooled. "Who were you thinking of, Jules?"

"What about Slade?"

"Slade?"

"He's nice." She tugged the frayed sleeves of her hoodie down, over her hands. "And he likes us."

"Us?" The word squeezed her heart.

She nodded and pushed her toast around the plate. "Yeah. He likes hanging out with us and…"

"What?" Beth prodded gently when Jules didn't continue.

"I'm not a little kid anymore, Mom." Beth held her breath. "It's okay if you date, like Auntie Sam."

Instinctively, Beth shook her head. She wasn't like Sam. Far from it.

"You can, Mom." Jules looked up from her plate and held her gaze. "You should. And Slade—"

"Is a musician, kiddo. He travels with his band. He's not the type of guy who settles down in a small town and—"

"He said it feels like home here," Jules blurted out.

Her heart stopped for a moment while she tried to process what her daughter had just said. "What?"

"He said Cedar Springs felt like home. That traveling got old, and it was nice to come back to a place that felt like home."

What could she say to that? Even if Slade had said that, he hadn't said it to her. And he certainly hadn't told her that he had any intention of staying in Cedar Springs or with her. But he hadn't said he wouldn't either.

"Look at the time." Beth jumped up from the table and poured the rest of her coffee in the sink. "We better get moving or we're going to be late."

HE SHOULD HAVE MADE the call the night before, but after dinner with Mona, Slade had picked up the phone, stared at Max's name and number, and couldn't make the call. Maybe the woman had a point. Maybe he did owe it to himself to think long and hard about what he wanted, but more importantly, what he needed.

The problem was, even after a night of thinking, playing his guitar and thinking some more, he still wasn't any closer to understanding his wants or needs. But he was out of time. As one last procrastination, Slade hopped in the shower and hoped maybe the water would give him a little clarity. But even as he wrapped the towel around his waist, he was no closer to an answer.

Still dripping wet, Slade picked up his cell phone and dialed Max's number. There was no point putting it off. He knew deep down what he had to do and all he was doing was killing time, and putting off the inevitable. The problem with what Mona had told him to think about was that he already knew the answers; he just didn't want to admit them.

What he wanted was Beth.

What he needed was for her to want him back.

She didn't.

The phone rang in his ear as the call connected. "Slade." Max's voice rang across the line. "I didn't expect to hear from you for a few days. You made that clear the other day."

"Yeah, well. Things change." He ran a hand through his wet hair and slicked it back. "Did you listen to the songs?"

"Did I? They're frickin' fantastic, Slade. The melodies are bang on." He should have been relieved to hear that Max liked his work. But strangely, Slade didn't feel much of anything when he got the other man's approval. "And different," Max continued. "Really different from what you've done before. But I like it," he added quickly.

"Have you let the guys listen?"

Max hesitated. "No," he said after a moment. "I think maybe you should be the one to show them the new songs. Run it through with them. They're a bit of a different direction for the Jacked Crackers. You might want to ease the guys into them. I don't know if...well, don't worry about it."

"What?"

"It's nothing. It's just the guys were talking and thinking maybe that you're done with…it doesn't matter."

It did matter. But not as much as it probably should have. Slade knew the guys had been thinking breakup for a while. And when he'd left, there was no doubt they'd thought that was it. They weren't stupid; they knew Slade was feeling restless. It didn't surprise him that they thought that he was done with the group. It wasn't that farfetched.

"You're coming back?" Max's question brought Slade back to the conversation.

That was the moment. The moment that Slade needed to tell him to book him a car to the airport and the next flight out, away from Cedar Springs. "I…"

He couldn't make himself say the words. He squeezed his eyes shut and rubbed the bridge of his nose hard, trying desperately to force himself to say the words.

"Slade? You're ready to meet us in Tampa, man? I sent everyone home for a rest, but that's the next stop on the tour. If you're ready, that is."

Tampa.

Slade let that sink in. Tampa was a long way away from Cedar Springs. It might as well have been a world away.

"Slade? I can get a car there in an hour. I'll get you on the—"

"No."

"No?"

He hadn't realized he'd said the word, made his decision, until Max repeated it.

"No," Slade said again, this time with conviction. "I'm not ready to go. I think you're right. The songs aren't right for the Jacked Crackers. They're more of a solo style. But I'm not done writing yet."

"What? Slow down." No doubt Max paced his office,

trying to wrap his brain around the new loop Slade had just thrown him. "What are you saying?"

He took a deep breath, and this time the words came easy. "I'm saying I'm done, Max. I'll call Axel and tell him myself, but it's time for a change."

"You have more songs to write?"

"Yes." His mind drifted to Beth: her perfect lips, her curves that fit his hands just right, the way she said his name. His real name. "But first I have something really important to do."

He ended the call and got dressed quickly. He pulled a pair of jeans on and picked a clean t-shirt from the suitcase he'd never unpacked. He needed Beth to want him, and even if she didn't realize it yet, he was going to make dammed sure she did.

Chapter Twelve

JULES WENT to school without any problem. Probably because she was excited to tell her friends about her little adventure, despite the fact that both Beth and Rhys had warned her about the risks of glamorizing a running away incident, no matter how it turned out. But Beth wasn't naive enough to think Jules would listen—she was twelve, after all— and sometimes that "twelve" looked a lot more like sixteen. She could only hope that Jules wouldn't forget to leave out the part where she was terrified at the truck stop and wanted to go home. There was something to be said for getting back into routine, but Beth had to fight her instinct to wrap Jules up in a protective bubble and keep her home just a little bit longer.

Rhys had assured Beth he'd stop in and check up on her as well as talk to the school principal, and perhaps address the entire student body on the risks associated with running away. It couldn't hurt.

What would hurt was if Beth was late for work, after everything that had gone down the day before. She could hope her bosses would be understanding, but even though Trent and Dylan were friends of hers, the Harrison brothers also ran a business. And if word got out about her and Slade…well, she didn't even want to think about it. The best defense was to get into work early and do her job to the best of her ability.

That was Beth's plan, anyway. As it turned out, she didn't get farther than the staff room before Carmen stopped her.

"Good morning," Beth said, trying for casual. "How are you feeling?" She gestured to Carmen's swelling belly and made a mental note to talk more with Sam about a baby shower for their friend. She'd been so caught up in her own dramas, she'd forgotten all about their plan.

"I'm doing fine, thank you." Carmen's hand went instinctively to her stomach. "But I do need to speak with you, Beth. Could you come with me?"

She knew what was coming, although she'd expected it from Trent because he was in charge of staff. Regardless, Beth knew she wasn't going to like the conversation. "I have a client in fifteen minutes, so I—"

Carmen nodded slightly. "I know. Josh will take it today."

That was a bad sign. A really bad sign. Someone must have said something. Kari? She'd said she wouldn't, but…it didn't matter. The fact was even if Kari hadn't said anything—which she probably didn't—the Springs was a small place; someone else would have found out. She'd been reckless, not thinking at all of the consequences. But Slade had that effect on her, which was yet another reason she needed to stay away from him.

Or run towards him, the voice in her head screamed.

Carmen didn't say another word until they were in her office with the door shut. Then it was Beth who started the conversation. "You get to do the honors, I guess?"

Her friend's smile was sympathetic. "Beth, don't think the worst. Please."

Beth shrugged. If she was going to get fired, she was going to do her best not to be upset by it. And strangely enough, she wasn't upset. She knew she should be. Hell, she should be terrified of the idea that she might be without a job. But surprisingly, the idea was kind of freeing. Like she might have options.

"Trent thought it was best if I spoke to you," Carmen said. "I think he felt a bit awkward given the circumstances and that we're all friends and…"

"It's okay."

"It's not okay, Beth." Carmen looked more serious than Beth had ever seen her. Genuine concern and worry lined her face. "Trent is quite upset that you were with a guest in the hot pools and—"

"I was doing therapy with him." Her excuse sounded lame. "On his wrist."

Carmen cocked her head and raised an eyebrow. "Therapy is to be confined to the treatment pools," she said. "You know that."

Beth nodded.

"You should know that Kari tried to cover for you."

That surprised her. "What?"

"Trent was informed of your…indiscretion…by one of the housekeeping staff. Turns out she's a bit of a Slade Black groupie and has been following his every move. She was only too happy to report you."

Beth groaned, but couldn't be angry. She deserved whatever punishment she had coming to her. "So? This is it, I guess."

"You're not losing your job, Beth."

The words echoed around the room and took Beth off guard.

"But we do have to suspend you for two weeks."

"Two weeks." She let that sink in and then nodded slowly. "That sounds fair." It was more than fair and they both knew it. But it didn't make it any easier to swallow. It was a good thing she had savings.

Together they walked to the door, but before Carmen

opened it, she turned to her friend. "Can I give you a bit of advice? As a friend, I mean."

"Of course."

"Why don't you spend a little time figuring out exactly why you were so willing to risk everything to be with Slade yesterday?" Beth wasn't stupid; she knew Carmen had heard about her blowup at the Grizzly Paw. If there was one thing she knew, it was that nothing was a secret in Cedar Springs. Not for long. "In my experience," Carmen continued, "people only take risks like that when something really matters. Or someone," she added with a sly smile. "And hey, it's not like you don't have a little spare time on your hands right now."

Despite everything, Beth smiled and hugged her friend before she left the office.

She made her way slowly down the hall and gave herself over to her jumbled thoughts. It was too hard to figure out what to do. Maybe she'd been right all along. Slade wasn't good for her. Didn't almost losing her job prove that? But it hadn't been Slade's fault, not really. She was the one who decided to take him up to the hot springs. And she'd known exactly what she risked. Maybe Carmen was right. It wasn't like her to act as impulsively as she had the day before, but being with Slade brought out all kinds of feelings she wasn't used to. And maybe it was time she explored those feelings.

TAKING a chance that Beth would be at work, Slade ran down the corridor towards the treatment rooms. He didn't stop to think about the consequences of interrupting her, or that he might get her in trouble. He couldn't think of anything except finding her and telling her that he wasn't going to walk away. Hell, he wasn't going anywhere unless she was with him. He'd never been so sure of anything before in his life.

He flung open the glass door of the physiotherapy rooms and a startled Josh looked up from the desk. "Beth. I need to—"

"She's not here today," Josh said. "She'll be out for a few weeks."

"A few weeks?"

"I can take a look at your—"

"No." They both knew Slade wasn't there for his wrist. "Where is she? Did she go on holiday?"

Josh shook his head and leaned across the desk to whisper. "She was suspended."

"Suspended?" Slade shouted the word, not caring who heard. "Why?" Realization crashed over him. "Because of me? Because of…" He didn't finish his thought. There was no time. He spun around and broke into a jog. He headed for the lobby and hopefully someone could lend him a car. He needed to get to Beth.

He didn't make it to the lobby before he saw a familiar blond making her way slowly down the hall. His heart sped up as he reached her. He grabbed her arm and spun her around to face him.

"Beth." Slade fought to catch his breath and slow his heart rate. "I'm sorry."

Her features turned from shock at being accosted in the hallway to confusion. "Sorry?"

"For getting you suspended." He knew he should say more. He knew what he really should say was that he wasn't sorry at all, that he'd do it again if it meant a chance to be with her. He'd break all the rules for her. Over and over again.

She gave him a small smile. "You didn't get me suspended. I did. It wasn't your fault."

"I'm still sorry. I shouldn't—"

"I'm not."

He hadn't released her arm, reluctant to let go of her, and

when she reached over and placed her free hand on top of his, Slade had to resist the urge to pull her to him. The need to be with her was intense.

"You're not?"

She shook her head. "No. I screwed up. I deserved it. And I should be the one to apologize to you." She squeezed his hand and he had to force himself to focus on what she said. "I was a jerk to you yesterday. You brought my baby home to me, and it wasn't your fault and—"

Slade put a finger on her lips. "You don't need to explain. You were scared and upset and...it's okay." Beth shook her head, and tried to open her mouth to argue with him, but Slade replaced his finger with his lips and swallowed her protests with the heat of his kiss.

"So what are you going to do with your time off?" Slade still held her close.

"I think it's going to give me some much-needed time to think about things and maybe make some decisions." She took a step back. Reluctantly, Slade let her go, but kept a hold on her arm. He wasn't going to let her go far. Not again.

"Decisions like whether you might want to come on a little trip with me while I officially break up with my band?"

She raised an eyebrow in question.

"I've been making some decisions, too."

"Oh yeah?" The corners of her lips curled up into a smile. "And what are they?"

"I think it's time for me to go solo." He let one hand trail up the inside of her arm; he drew her closer as he spoke. "At least as far as my music goes." Slade stared directly into her eyes as he spoke. He needed her to understand exactly what he was saying. "It'll also give me a lot more time to work on some new collaborations."

"Really?"

He nodded. "I don't have it fully worked out yet. But I

think we both owe it to ourselves to see where it could go, because I think it could be pretty great."

"I don't know." She shook her head, but he saw the smile she tried to hide. "A rock star and a small-town mom? It's crazy."

"Crazy enough to work."

She nodded and let a small smile play on her lips. "I think you might be right, Slade Black."

He couldn't resist her any longer. One hand cupped the back of her head and he pulled her into him. He crushed her mouth with his, drunk in every bit of the sweetness her lips offered him. She met his kiss with an urgency of her own, and when he pulled back, he looked directly into her clear blue eyes when he said, "I've never been more right about anything."

Epilogue

IT HAD BEEN JUST over a month since Beth and Slade had left for Los Angeles so Slade could record some early tracks for his new solo album. It had surprised everyone when Beth decided to take time off work to join him. But she couldn't imagine being anywhere else.

Even Jules had joined them for a week of spring break before returning home to stay with Sam and Trent until Slade had things wrapped up. Not for the first time, Beth was grateful for having good friends to support her.

As much as she'd enjoyed her time away, there was no way Beth would have missed Carmen's baby shower.

The banquet room at the Springs resort might have seemed like an extravagant place for most people to hold a baby shower, but for Carmen and Dylan it was absolutely perfect. The early March sun shone through the wall of windows; the entire room was lit up and warm, and the fact that at eight months pregnant, Carmen was simply glowing certainly didn't hurt either.

Carmen and Dylan had made a lot of friends in the short time they'd been at the Springs, and everyone loved them, so it wasn't a surprise that the room was packed. A table off to the side overflowed with presents and the guests of honor soaked up the attention in the center of the room, surrounded by a group of mostly women, while the men hovered around the food table.

As she moved through the room, Beth fielded all kinds of questions but finally made her way across the room to her friend. "I can't believe how big you've gotten in the last few weeks." Beth's hand dropped to her friend's stomach and patted it lovingly. "You look amazing, Carmen."

The women embraced, and both of them ended up wiping a tear from their cheeks. "I'm so glad you made it back for the shower." Carmen clasped Beth's hand and pulled her down into the chair recently vacated by Dylan. "I thought you'd be too busy jet-setting in LA."

"Stop it," Beth laughed. "I'd never miss this. Besides, I missed Jules too much. I wanted her to stay with us, but she insisted it was time to go home."

Slade laughed. "For a girl who wanted to travel so badly, she sure missed home and her new friends. But we did get her to agree to come to Europe with us for a few weeks this summer."

"Europe?"

Beth nodded in answer to Carmen's question, her smile wide on her face. "Isn't it exciting? Slade's manager wants to do some early release events over there for his new solo album. He thinks the Europeans are going to love it."

"Everyone's going to love it." Dylan slapped his buddy on the back. "And it's good to see you so happy, man."

Beth couldn't disagree with that. She winked and blew Slade a kiss.

"Come on," Dylan said to Slade. "Let's leave the ladies alone. Jax said he had a *thing* to show me." He looked at

Carmen who shook her head and smiled. Both of them knew there was no *thing*.

"Go." she laughed and swatted Dylan away. "I'm fine and I know this isn't your scene anyway."

He leaned down and kissed Carmen on the cheek. "I'll be right over there if you need anything."

"I'm not going into labor, don't worry. Besides, I'm in good hands here."

But before they could make their escape, Jax Carver found them.

LOADED up with a full platter of canapés, Jax wove his way through the crowd to rescue his boss and friend from the baby shower. "It looks like this group could use some more food." He lowered the tray so the women could fill their plates. "And when you have a minute…" He looked toward the men. "Dylan, I wanted to show you the…"

"Thing?" Dylan perked up and Carmen just laughed.

"Yes." Jax nodded slowly and shifted the tray. "The *thing* needs our attention. Why don't you guys come and—"

"Just go," Beth interrupted them before they could carry on any further. "I'm more than happy to hang out with the mother to be."

Jax lifted the tray and after the others gave their women quick kisses, they made their way to the other side of the room where Rhys and Trent were chatting. "Here," Jax said as he pushed the tray between them and onto the table. "Try these. And look who I found."

The men all greeted Slade the way men do, with back slaps and insults, but it was obvious they were happy to have their friend back. Even Rhys, who'd taken a little longer to warm up to Slade because of his close relationship with Beth, had accepted him into their group. Besides, no one could deny that it was kind of fun to have a rock star for a friend, especially when he made Beth so happy.

"So, it's about time that you returned my star physiotherapist," Trent teased. "Things are starting to get busy now for the summer season ramping up. I'm going to need her a lot more."

"About that—"

"Don't say it," Trent warned. "Do not tell me you're moving away. I thought you liked it here."

"I do," Slade said quickly. "We do. But we will be traveling and Beth was going to talk to you about maybe a part-time schedule…"

Trent and Dylan both sighed and shook their heads. Trent looked like he was about to object, but at the last minute shook his head. "I'm sure we can figure something out, but we'll talk about it later. Aren't we supposed to be playing some games involving diapers or something?"

Everyone laughed and Jax used the opportunity to escape to the kitchen. "I better go reload," he said as way of an excuse as he lifted his mostly empty tray. "This is a hungry crowd and I want to make sure everyone's well fed before the cake comes out."

"We have staff for that. Why don't you go get changed and come and join the party for real?" Dylan was a good friend. Not that he'd had much time to get to know anybody as well as he'd like. Since coming to the Springs, he was always so busy making sure the kitchen ran smoothly, or that the new recipes he worked on were going to be well received, that he didn't have much time for friends, or relationships.

"I appreciate it, man." Jax shook his head. "But I like to take a hands-on approach, make sure everything is going smoothly."

"Don't we know it." Trent nodded in appreciation. "But

you know you can have a little fun, too, right? All work and no play is…well…boring. Samantha taught me that."

Rhys laughed. "Coming from the two biggest workaholics I know, that's pretty funny."

"Well," Trent said. "It's true. You have to slow down and enjoy life sometimes."

Jax slipped to the side. "I'll tell you what," he said. "I'll relax later. When the party's over." He made his escape before his friends could protest further and headed into the kitchen, his sanctuary.

He'd spent his entire adult life working on his career; it was important to him. No, more than important. It was everything. At least it had been. He put the tray down, so one of the waitresses could reload it, and he made his way around the room to check on everything.

Everything looked good. He had to admit, everything had gone off without a hitch and that's because his staff was top-notch. Everything about the Springs was. When he'd landed this job, he'd thrived with the challenge it offered, the constant opportunity for growth and development; it was his dream job. But they'd been open almost a year, and everything was going smoothly. Dammit. He did deserve a bit of fun. It'd been way too long since he'd sat down and had a beer with the guys.

Jax wiped his hands on a towel and tossed it in a bin. "You have this under control, Brent?"

His sous chef nodded. "Of course. You takin' off?"

"I think so. I'll see you tomorrow, okay?"

He left the kitchen behind him and headed towards the back hallway that would take him to staff quarters, where he could go change and then take Dylan up on his offer to join the party as a guest. After all, it was unlikely that everything would go to hell in the kitchen on a Sunday afternoon. Especially with the training he'd given his crew.

Before he could reach the exit, a loud voice caught his

attention. A female voice. And she didn't sound happy. With most of the management at the baby shower, Jax instinctively turned and jogged towards the voice that rose in volume.

When he got to the lobby, he froze and watched the scene in front of him. A tall brunette, her arms waving, stood in the middle of the lobby. Her voice rose in volume as she spoke to Sara one of the front desk employees.

"I want to speak to my grandmother," she said. "I know she's here, so you might as well just tell me what room she's in."

"We called her room, ma'am. She's not—"

"I'm not a ma'am."

"Oh…I'm…"

She was definitely not a ma'am. She was gorgeous and the way she was getting worked up, was incredibly hot. Jax knew he should step in and help out Sara, but he was having way too much fun watching.

"My name is Bria Sheridan and my grandmother is a guest here. I demand to speak with her before she's conned out of spending one more dime here."

"We're doing our best to contact her, Ms. Sheridan. But I can't let you—"

For Jax, that was his cue to step in. "Hey." He held his hands up and stepped between the women. "Is there a problem here?"

The second the woman whirled around to look at him, Jax felt a twist in his gut and momentarily forgot what he planned to do. She was stunning and with her dark eyes blazing with anger, Jax's imagination took a twist. He couldn't help but wonder if those eyes would look the same fueled by passion looking up at him as he—

"And who the hell are you?"

What is Bria so worked up about? Can Jax calm her down or will he only fan the flames in a fire that might be hot enough to burn them both? Find out now in Midnight Springs!

You can read a special excerpt right after this—>

I appreciate you helping me spread the word about the books you love! Reviews help readers discover their next favorite read! Please leave a review on your favorite book retailer!

Don't forget to join my mailing list where you'll be the first to hear about new stories, sales and promotions and giveaways! You can join me here —>
https://elenaaitken.com/newsletter/

Midnight Springs

Please enjoy an excerpt from Midnight Springs.

IT HAD ONLY BEEN a little more than an hour since Bria Sheridan had been accompanied up to what was a very fancy room at the Springs hotel. The management said they would comp the room, and so they should for all the money they were swindling out of her grandmother, Mona. A flash of guilt flared through her when she replayed the scene she'd caused in the lobby. She hadn't really planned to let things get so out of hand when she'd arrived at the resort and they wouldn't tell her where her grandmother was. But she also hadn't planned to go and personally haul her grandmother out of there. At least not until the night before, when Mona told her over the phone that she'd be staying at least for the next two months. No way was Bria going to stand for that. Besides, until her latest photo assignment was finished and accepted, she didn't really have anywhere else to go. It seemed like a good solution.

The Springs billed themselves as a place with magic healing waters, but all Bria could see was an overpriced spa that prayed on the elderly who only wanted a miracle they couldn't have—no matter how much money they spent. At least she'd gotten there when she had; who knows how much money she'd saved her grandma from spending. But first she had to convince her tough-as-nails grandma of that.

There was a sharp knock at the door and Bria didn't even have to guess who it was. She doubted very much it was room service coming to bring her complimentary champagne and strawberries.

"Speak of the devil," she muttered as she opened the door. Her face transformed into what had to look like a very fake smile. "Grandma." She held her arms out to her favorite relative, but Mona only pushed past her into the room.

"Don't you Grandma me, young lady. Do you know what it's like to walk out of a therapeutic treatment where some handsome yet unseen young man with fingers like a god made me feel like a young woman again, only to be met by a security guard who tells you that your favorite granddaughter has just made a scene to end all scenes and has been escorted to a room where she's waiting to speak to me? Do you have any idea what that's like? Because it's kind of a buzzkill."

Instead of feeling chastised as she probably should have, Bria stuck her chin up and put her hands on her hips. "This is crazy, Grandma. This place is taking advantage of you."

"They're not and I can't believe they'd give you a room after the tantrum you likely had in the lobby. What they should have done was call Rhys Anderson and escort you to the Cedar Springs jailhouse."

Bria had to bite back a laugh at her grandmother's choice of words. "First of all, I don't think they call them jailhouses anymore. And second of all, you've clearly been here too long if you know the name of the local police officer. Or have you been the one who's had to visit the jailhouse recently?"

Bria hoped her lighter tone would defuse the tension. She hated there to be any bad feelings between them. Especially if she was going to convince her grandma to leave this place before it bankrupted her.

Just as she thought it would, Mona's shoulders relaxed and her face split into a smile. "Well, however you got here, you're here and I can't think of anyone I'd rather see. Besides, you come by that attitude naturally." Mona winked and held out her arms. "Come give your grandma a hug."

Bria let herself get pulled into her grandmother's embrace. It had always been her favorite place to be: her safe place, long after she should have been too old. She inhaled deeply; her childhood self hoped to get a lungful of her grandma's warm cinnamon fragrance that always reminded her of fresh baking. But it wasn't there. Instead, it was a pungent oil that filled her senses: a heady mixture of musk and flowers and something that was distinctly not her grandmother. Bria pulled away abruptly and tried to mask her shock.

"You're too thin." Mona pushed past her into Bria's posh room. She walked right past the pillow bed where Bria had dumped her small suitcase, and directly to a door she hadn't noticed before.

"Isn't Carmen clever?"

"Carmen?"

"The customer service manager, remember?" Mona rolled her eyes when Bria nodded. She'd met so many people since she'd stormed through the front doors of the Springs. They'd all been friendly, too. Starting with the very good-looking and slightly cocky—okay, really cocky—dirty blond, slightly scruffy in a way-too-handsome way guy. He'd thrown her off her game a little, which was probably a good thing considering she'd been behaving like a first-class brat. Even she could admit that. She blushed slightly with the memory.

"I remember. The pregnant one," Bria admitted. "Why is she so clever?"

Mona twisted the handle and pulled the door open to

reveal a room behind it. "She put us in adjoining rooms." Her grandmother lit up in a smile. "And wait until you see my suite."

"Suite?" Bria groaned at the thought of how much a suite would cost her grandmother in such a fancy place. She followed her through the door. "Do you really need a whole..." Her objections died on her lips as she took in the room.

Although Bria had been impressed with her own accommodations, her grandmother's suite was ten times bigger and fancier.

"It's pretty nice, right?"

Nice was an understatement, and by the look on her grandmother's face, she knew it too. Bria walked around the space. Her fingers trailed over the smooth polished wood of the dining table, the granite countertop of the kitchen and the... wait a minute. The kitchen?

"Why do you need a room with a kitchen in it?"

It was no secret that Mona didn't cook. Not even a little bit. It was a family joke that she could barely even heat up soup without burning it. The only time Mona ever set foot in a kitchen was for her once-a-year cinnamon bun extravaganza. It was a tradition ever since Bria was a little girl that her grandma would spend an entire day, from dawn until well into the night, mixing, rolling, rising, and icing cinnamon buns. They were always best fresh out of the oven and everyone who knew about it seemed to casually drop by that day to get a taste of her famous buns. But whatever wasn't eaten was frozen and brought out over the course of the year. Bria could never figure out why she insisted on only baking once a year when everyone so clearly loved her cinnamon buns, and she was so good at it, but her grandma insisted that by not doing it all the time, it remained special and people cared about it. There was some logic in that, Bria supposed, but as a little girl, all she could think of was the taste of the warm sticky bun in her mouth and the lingering scent that always seemed to cling to her grandma, even months after she'd cooked her last bun. The scent that was so obviously missing when Bria hugged her.

When was the last time her grandmother had baked? Was her arthritis really so bad?

Her grandma waved away the question. "This is how all the suites come. I usually take my meals in the restaurant. You should taste Jax's food. He is a miracle worker."

Jax. The name seemed vaguely familiar. But there was no way she would have met him. Nor did she want to. Bria had no intention to stay at the resort for one moment longer than necessary.

Not that there was anywhere else for her to go. The thought crossed her mind before she had a chance to block it.

"We'll have dinner down there and you can meet him. He's so funny and very talented in the kitchen, of course. Such a nice young man. Really, they are all so pleasant here at the Springs. I met the loveliest young guitar player. Simon Black, but he called himself something else. I don't know why. The name Simon is perfectly good and—"

"Wait." Bria held up a hand to slow her grandma and her rambling trail of thoughts so she could catch up. "Black? You mean, Slade Black?"

There had been some sort of rumor about the famous guitar player who'd left his band and started up a solo career after falling in love with a single mom in a small town. "No way." All the pieces fell together. "That was here? And you met him?"

Her grandmother stood straight and patted her hair. "Not only did I meet him, but some would say I was instrumental in his life." She waggled her eyebrows and smirked.

Bria couldn't help it; she burst out laughing. "Of course you were, Grandma."

"You'll see. You stick around here long enough and I'll even help you, my dear."

The laughter died on Bria's lips. There was no help for her. She'd made sure of that. With her career on life support and her personal life little more than nonexistent, there wasn't much to help. But she wouldn't fail at everything. She took another look around the opulent surroundings; her gaze rested back on her grandma. No. She'd save her grandma from making the biggest mistake of her life and throwing her life savings down the drain. That she could do.

———

THE KITCHEN BUZZED with the usual dinner prep insanity. Something about a restaurant kitchen inspired chaos. No matter how much planning or preparation head chef Jax Carver had put into it, something inevitably went wrong.

"Chef. I can't find the mushrooms."

Jax looked up from the bowl where he'd been preparing a dry rub for the night's special. "What kind of mushrooms?" His latest hire, Doug, was a good kid, but some days Jax felt more like he was babysitting then preparing food.

"The white ones."

"Button mushrooms?"

Doug looked confused for a moment, and then nodded. "Yup. Those ones. I need them for the soup."

Jax forced himself to take a deep breath. "How many times have I told you, we don't—"

"I got this, Chef." Brent appeared out of nowhere and deftly slid between Jax and the prep cook. "Doug, we've been through this. There are five kinds of mushrooms in the soup, none of which are button mushrooms. Come on, I'll show you. Again."

Brent winked at Jax over his shoulder as he led the kid

away, and Jax made a mental note to buy his assistant head chef a drink later to thank him for doing such a good job.

The truth was, ever since Jax had gotten Stillwater up and running, he'd slowly started to pull back from the daily operations, allowing Brent more and more responsibility. Stillwater had been a hit, just like everything at the Springs resort had been. Sure, it had taken a lot of hard work and menu planning as he fine-tuned exactly what the upscale clientele would like to eat. But Jax had a knack for knowing exactly how to put dishes together. He was an expert at planning and creating a winning menu. But once he'd done that...where was the challenge?

Jax went back to his preparations with a sigh. That was the whole problem, the one that had eaten away at him for the last few months. He was getting bored again, which meant he'd want to move on to the next challenge, as was his pattern. No time to worry about that now, he thought as he added some cayenne to the bowl and mixed. For now, he'd focus on the dinner rush. He'd think about what he was going to do next later. Especially if his application at Angles, the latest hot spot in Los Angeles, was accepted. He mailed it off two weeks ago, which in of itself was strange, since he couldn't remember the last time anyone actually used the mail system. As well as being old school, the chef who ran the new venture was famous for leaving everything until the last minute, even so, Jax had hoped to hear by now.

"Hey. Is this a bad time?" The Harrison brothers Trent and Dylan walked through the gleaming stainless-steel kitchen toward him.

"Never a bad time for you two." Not for the owners of the Springs, Jax thought. But more than his bosses, they were good guys and the closest thing to real friends Jax had had in years. Moving around from restaurant to restaurant in as many cities didn't really allow for close friendships, which, for the most part, Jax was fine with. He'd never been one for guys nights and shooting the shit. Relationships of any kind were way more work than they were worth.

"What happened to you last night?" Trent lounged against the counter and grabbed a bun from the bread basket nearby. "I thought you were going to come back and join us after the baby shower thing. Not that it wasn't a lot of fun and all, Dyl." He shot his brother a glance and dodged the subsequent punch in the shoulder his brother delivered.

Jax had forgotten all about promising to meet up with the guys. He'd catered the baby shower for Dylan and his very pregnant girlfriend, Carmen, who happened to be the customer service manager at the Springs. After the party, he actually had agreed to go out and have a drink, which was unusual in itself, but what was even more unusual was being distracted by the very beautiful and extremely fired-up woman in the lobby when he'd gone to change. He grinned at the memory of the feisty brunette who'd been on a rant in the lobby the night before. He'd done his best to calm her down, but it was ultimately Carmen who'd shown up to smooth the waters. Jax had gone back to his apartment and forgotten all about drinks with the guys.

"I must have fallen asleep." It was a lie, but they didn't need to know that he'd been so distracted by a woman that he'd blown them off. "Sorry. Another time." Another lie. He'd already decided he shouldn't build their friendship any more than he already had. It would only make it harder to leave. And he was going to leave. He just needed to figure out when and where he'd go next.

Dylan nodded but eyed him suspiciously. "You alright?"

"Why wouldn't I be?"

Dylan was about to say something else, but Trent cut him off. "Of course he's alright. Don't be such a girl. Hanging out with your hormonal woman is making you sensitive."

Jax laughed but Dylan raised his eyebrows. "You'd say that to her face, would you?"

"You know I wouldn't."

They all laughed and Jax felt his mood lighten the way it always did around the Harrison brothers. The sound of a clanging pot brought him back to the present. He still had a dinner rush to prepare for. "What's up, guys? I know you didn't come here just to check on my feelings. Not that I don't appreciate it and all, but I do have to get back to work."

"True," Dylan said. "Your boss is a real dick."

Trent shoved him and stepped forward to hand Jax a piece of paper.

"What's this?"

"Augustus Bernstein," Trent said by way of explanation. And it was all the explanation he needed. Jax snatched the piece of paper and unfolded it, quickly scanning the text.

He had to read it twice before he looked up at Trent. "Augustus Bernstein? He's coming here?"

Trent nodded with a shit-eating grin on his face. "Pretty cool, right?"

"Don't let him take all the credit for it," Dylan jumped in. "I sent the request."

"Details, details." Trent waved his brother's protests away. "Either way, he's coming. Here. And you're going to impress him. Not only that, but with an Augustus Bernstein review, we'll be able to get some national and hopefully international media coverage for your amazing cuisine. Think of the boon for business."

Jax's mind spun. He'd always wanted to be reviewed by Augustus Bernstein. He was only the most notable food critic in North America. He was also notoriously selective about what restaurants he reviewed. And he was tough, too. But a review from Augustus would make his career. He could go anywhere. Cook anywhere. His career would be made.

And for a man who liked to be on the move...

"Wow," was all he could manage.

"Yeah, wow. More than wow. And he's coming next month, so you have a little bit of time to prepare."

"Next month?"

A month was not enough time. He'd have to plan a menu, test it and refine it. A month was not enough time for that.

"Well, three weeks, actually."

Jax looked up, mouth hanging open, and stared at Dylan, who'd just spoken.

"Three weeks?"

"It's all we could get and we were lucky to get that..."

Jax stopped listening as Dylan and Trent congratulated themselves on their achievement and what would ultimately be one of the biggest determining factors in Jax's career.

Now he just had to figure out how to make sure that was a positive thing.

———

CAUGHT up in the mania of the dinner rush, Jax didn't have much time to think about the letter and impending visit from Augustus Bernstein, which was a good thing because once he started to think about it, he didn't think he'd be able to stop. As it was, he was effectively able to push it from his mind and focus on pushing out perfectly plated and prepared meals.

On the last ticket, Jax wiped the rim of the plate, put it up in the window and breathed a sigh of relief. A few orders would trickle in for the rest of the night, but nothing his staff couldn't handle. He was just about to untie his apron strings when Sarah, one of the waitresses, appeared to pick up the food.

"Thanks, Jax. It looks great." She picked up the plates and as an afterthought, turned to him. "Oh, and there's someone at table six who wants to speak to the chef. She was very demanding." Sarah winked at him and Jax knew right away who it was.

Mona, the spunky guest they'd all come to think of as their resident grandmother, liked to personally thank Jax for every meal. She didn't always request to see him during the dinner rush, though. She was a smart woman, and knew enough to pull him away from the kitchen when it wasn't very busy and he could safely get away. Hell, even if he couldn't, he would for her. Something about the older woman made him happy. If only he could find that in a woman his own age...nah, who was he kidding? Even if by some miracle he found a woman who challenged him enough to keep him interested for more than one or two weeks, he'd never settle down. That would mean being tied to one place, and he'd seen firsthand with his own family growing up how damaging it could be to put all your eggs in one basket. He wouldn't make that mistake.

"Should I tell her you'll be out when you get a minute?" He'd forgotten Sarah was still there.

"No." He gestured to the steaming plates of food she held. "You take those out and I'll go say hi."

Sarah smiled and took off to deliver the food. Jax gave the counter a final wipe, left the kitchen in Brent's capable hands and took off his apron, throwing it into the laundry bin before he changed his mind last minute and circled back to the walk-in refrigerator. The pastry chef had worked on some new desserts, and he couldn't think of anyone better to spoil with a fresh piece of cheesecake. After he added a mint leaf and a raspberry for a garnish, Jax made his way out to the dining room with a smile.

Mona sat in her usual spot. It was crazy to think that a guest could have a usual spot, but she'd been at the Springs so long, she was starting to become a fixture. But what did it mean if he was getting attached to her? Just another reason he needed to leave soon. It was time to move on if he was getting attached. It always hurt less to take off sooner rather than later. And sometimes it did hurt. Leaving the Springs would be one of those times.

But he couldn't think about it yet. Especially not with the Augustus review looming. He'd sort it out. Later. First, Jax was determined to enjoy a bit of dessert with his favorite lady.

"I hear there was someone here who wanted to talk to the chef," Jax said as seriously as he could as he approached the table. "I hope there's not a problem with the—"

His words died on his lips as he noticed Mona was not alone. At first he hadn't noticed the striking brunette next to Mona, but he had seen her before: the night before in the lobby of the hotel, throwing what could only be equated to an adult tantrum.

"Oh. I'm sorry." Jax tried to keep his face as neutral as possible despite the fact that he desperately wanted to know why this beautiful and somewhat volatile woman sat with Mona. "I just assumed you were alone." He put the dessert in front of Mona and flashed an apologetic smile to the mysterious brunette, who watched him with a guarded look. It was an improvement: the last time he saw her, she'd been screaming at him. "I can get you a dessert, too, if you'd like?"

"Nonsense." Mona waved away his protests. "Jax, I want you to meet my granddaughter, Bria."

Granddaughter? The screaming tantrum started to make a little more sense in his mind as he remembered the way she'd been yelling about her...grandmother. Mona. It all made sense.

Well, not really. It actually didn't make any sense at all.

"It's nice to meet you." He held out his hand, choosing to assume she didn't remember him from the night before. Or at least, to give her a way out of what probably was an embarrassing situation for her.

"We've met." She raised one perfectly groomed eyebrow at

him but made no move to take his proffered hand. So, she was going to play it that way?

He couldn't help the smirk that pulled at his lips. He tucked his hand back in his pocket.

"How did you meet already?" A frown creased Mona's face. No doubt she'd been looking forward to making the introduction.

"I helped her—"

"He was—"

They spoke at the same time.

"After you."

Bria narrowed her dark eyes at him in a way that was probably supposed to come off as antagonistic, but Jax only found it incredibly sexy. Something about the woman, as angry and spirited as she clearly was, was also hot. Very hot.

She cleared her throat and pointedly looked away from Jax to focus on her grandmother. "I was just going to say that I met Jax last night when I arrived."

"Yes," Jax said as innocently as he could, enjoying the heat coming off the beautiful woman. "I'm just glad I was there to help out. Bria was very upset."

Mona's gaze flipped between them, a question in her eyes. Jax did his best to keep his face a careful mask of neutrality and as much as he wanted to, he didn't dare glance in Bria's direction. She didn't exactly seem like the kind of girl who'd appreciate being fooled with. But he couldn't help himself. It was too easy.

"Well, I do understand there was a bit of a fuss last night." Mona picked up a fork and slid it into the dessert. "I'm glad you were there for her, Jax."

He nodded solemnly.

"You know, Bria, Jax is very well thought of around here and it's always a good idea to have the best chef in town on your side." Mona winked at him and put the forkful in her mouth.

He couldn't help himself then, and he looked at Bria, whose pretty mouth, with her perfect lush lips, was turned down in a frown. He was pretty sure if her grandmother hadn't been next to her, she would have thrown her fork at his head, or something equally maiming. He winked at her at the exact moment that Mona let out a satisfied groan.

"This is so good, Jax." She shoved the plate toward her granddaughter. "You have to try this, Bria. Jax, you've really outdone yourself."

"I don't like dessert." Bria crossed her arms over her chest, which had the very fortunate side effect of pressing her breasts up to give Jax a generous view of her cleavage.

"Oh, I can't take any credit for the dessert. That's all Rose, my pastry chef."

"In that case," Bria smirked and she reached for the plate, "I think maybe I will give it a try."

He watched as she slid her fork into the creamy confection and put it in her mouth. His body reacted to the innocent action with a heat in his groin. He had no business having any kind of feeling for a woman who was so obviously angry about something, and clearly hated him on sight.

But there was no help for it; he was intrigued. Jax settled in and allowed himself to watch her reaction to the creamy deliciousness of the dessert. Bria had no idea the effect she had on him and she obviously had no idea that her face showed every little thing. Including how much she enjoyed her mouthful of sin.

Jax's mind flashed to a very different type of sin he could introduce that pretty mouth to, but Mona's presence snapped him back to reality.

"It's amazing, Jax. You tell Rose she has a winner." Mona

scooped up another bite before adding, "It's simply the most delicious thing I've ever tasted. Don't you think, Bria?"

Bria was quite obviously enjoying her own moment with the dessert. It was a rare thing when Jax saw someone enjoy food so thoroughly that they forgot where they were. It was incredible. And only served to make him want to get to know her even more. It took Bria a second to realize she was being spoken to but when she did, a blush crept over her cheeks.

"What?"

"I asked if you liked it." Mona's eyes danced with mischief. "But I think the better question would be if you wanted to be left alone with it."

Jax had to swallow a burst of laughter, and Bria's face burned brighter.

"Grandma!"

She shrugged and winked at Jax. "It was a fair question."

Bria's fork clattered to the plate and her face burned an even deeper red, but it was the flare in her blue eyes that intrigued Jax the most. He would have happily sat there all day, egging her on, but he had work to do—a lot of work, if he thought about the menu he'd need to prepare for the critic. Doing his best to suppress his smile, Jax pushed up from the table.

"It's been fun, ladies, but I should get going." His gaze locked on Bria, who'd managed to regain some of her composure. "I hope to see you again, Bria. How long will you be staying with us?"

"Not long." She straightened her shoulders and lifted her chin. Her long dark hair fell down her back. "I'll be taking my grandma and leaving just as soon as I—"

"Just hold on, young lady."

The two women glared at each other and it wasn't hard for Jax to see the family resemblance as far as the stubbornness was concerned. As much as he would have liked to stay and watch how the scene would play out, Jax was no fool when it came to women. Particularly angry women. He knew his cue to leave when he saw it.

He gave them each an easy smile and made his escape, but before he pushed the door back into the kitchen, he took one last look at the young woman who was now intensely arguing with her grandmother. Jax liked a challenge, and there was no doubt that's exactly what Bria would be.

Read the rest of Midnight Springs NOW!

About the Author

Elena Aitken is a USA Today Bestselling Author of more than forty romance and women's fiction novels. Living a stone's throw from the Rocky Mountains with her teenager twins, their two cats and a goofy rescue dog, Elena escapes into the mountains whenever life allows. She can often be found with her toes in the lake and a glass of wine in her hand, dreaming up her next book and working on her own happily ever after with her very own mountain man.

To learn more about Elena:
www.elenaaitken.com
elena@elenaaitken.com